Vodianoi

ALSO BY CHRIS MANNING

George and Condi: The Last Decayed. A Collection of Poems from the Last Decade

Beaver Tales and a Canada Goosing: Poems Illustrating a Uniquely Canadian Perspective

To the Shore of a Child's Ocean. Part One: Homeschooling from Birth to Age Nine

To the Shore of a Child's Ocean. Part Two: Homeschooling from Ages Nine to Fifteen

Vodianoi

CHRIS MANNING

APP
Artisan Pacific Publishing
Victoria, British Columbia
ArtisanPacificPublishing@gmail.com
sites.google.com/site/artisanpacificpublishing

Library and Archives Canada Cataloguing in Publication

Manning, Chris, 1965-
Vodianoi / Chris Manning.

ISBN 978-1-4636-4695-0

I. Title.

PS8626.A637V64 2011   jC813'.6   C2011-904922-8

Artisan Pacific Publishing
Victoria, British Columbia
ArtisanPacificPublishing@gmail.com
sites.google.com/site/artisanpacificpublishing

DEDICATION

To my family. Because of you I see magic wherever I go.

AUTHOR'S NOTE

What you are about to read was never meant to become a youth novel. Rather, it was intended as one chapter within the second installment of my homeschooling series entitled *To the Shore of a Child's Ocean*. But as sometimes happens during an active writing process, a metamorphosis of the project began to take place. Chapter Nine – *Vodianoi* (as it was called then) began to hum, to sparkle and eventually it seemed to burst into life, demanding to be shared with a younger audience. So after thoughtful consideration, I decided to heed the call and present *Vodianoi* as a companion novel to the original work but intended specifically for fantasy-loving young people. If after reading this novel you wish to learn more about the day-to-day homeschooling dynamics that occupied our protagonists during this time in their lives, please refer to Part Two of my homeschooling series.

VODIANOI

I

HI! I'M ALEX. I'm 12 and I'm a girl – I bet the name threw you off. It's short for Alexandra – a name that's just too stuffy for the likes of me. You could say I'm a bit of a free spirit. My mom says I'm a force to be reckoned with. True.

I'm going to tell you a story that you may not believe. I know my mom and dad didn't, but speaking for me and my brother Rick, we believe. He's a year younger than me and pretty much my best friend – when we're not plotting to kill each other, that is. Just kidding. But hey, you probably know what it's like with little brothers. We spend a lot of time together and share most everything and no one can drive me absolutely crazy like him. "Short trip," he says. Brothers!

Anyway, our adventure began that afternoon my friend, Rita found a really neat feather at the beach...

"Guys! Look at this!"

That's her. She and her brother, Jerry are homeschooled like Rick and me and they live just a couple blocks from us. She's 11 and he's 14. She's a bit of a musical prodigy. Pick an instrument, any instrument and she is liable to pick it up and make glorious music with it. He on the other hand, hasn't really found his niche in life yet but is an interesting guy nonetheless – as you'll see.

We get permission to go to the beach by ourselves pretty often – Mom says, "as long as we all stick together". I carry a cell phone for emergencies and I'd say we're pretty street-savvy.

We live on an island off the west coast of British Columbia, Canada. Green, lush and fresh. The beach is inevitably calling and combing its shores is almost a way of life here. It's always a good day to go to the beach – even when it rains. It rains a bit here. Ha! It rains a lot here but that doesn't stop any of us west coasters. We're not made of sugar.

"Whatcha got?" I was first to arrive as is my way.

"It's a feather but feel it. It's weird and well...wonderful!" Rita has a way of seeing everything in the best possible light. She's pretty easy to be around. And, she was right about that feather. It *was* beautiful...and odd. It was about 12 inches long and had a metallic golden sheen. It was etched with an intricate, shimmering, out-of-this-world kind of detail of elaborate whirls. It felt like the down of a lamb's ear.

"What kind of bird would have a feather like this?" Jerry had gingerly taken the feather from me and begun to examine it with his own brand of scientific zeal. He doesn't have the patience for simply admiring the beauty of things. Just the facts please ma'am. "It's the strangest thing".

Thwarted in his preliminary inspection, he handed the feather to Rick so he could take a stab at identifying it, but he couldn't figure it out either. "But wait, maybe..." He stopped. He appeared to be unlocking some hidden mystery, leafing through pages of complicated code within his mind. He took a deep breath. "What if it belongs to some kind of creepy alien bird that flew here from some bizarre planet called Icktorian and it's bent on taking over the world and ...?"

"Rick!" We cut him off before he could get too carried away – as is *his* way.

This was quite the conundrum. We had been coming to this same beach for years and, I guess almost through osmosis (oh yeah, and with our parents help), we know a lot about marine life, shells, tides, you name it. But this unusual find had us stumped. We decided to take the mystery feather back to our house to conduct a little more comprehensive research on it.

Leaving the beach, we enter a veritable rainforest, eclectic in Douglas fir, arbutus, red cedar and Garry oak covered in shrouds of moss and lichen. There is so much translucent green heavily draped over everything, sometimes you feel as though some of those greens have no business being so, well – green. As I walked, coastal birds provided a merry backdrop to my reverie in noisy, good natured chatter. And, although it wasn't raining, my outer layers became moist in sympathy to a mounting dampness. An unmistakably thick, woody, organic aroma emanated from the forest floor. Ah, September in the Pacific Northwest!

Ten minutes passed and we exited our dazzling coastal forest to encounter a somewhat less wooded area speckled with traces of civilization. Down a narrow, winding street to our home, we came across a hushed atmosphere of stillness flanked on both sides by majestic forest pillars. We walked up our drive and entered our two-storey, white stucco-with-avocado-green-trim home to discard our now slick all-weather gear. We washed up and moved upstairs to my bedroom to start up my computer. While it loaded, we leafed through some of our books on marine birds that we had in our home library, but to no avail. No matches. And when the computer was ready, a quick Internet search revealed little more.

"If this feather doesn't belong to any of the birds in all these books or on the net, what could it possibly come from?" Jerry appealed to the rest of us, but we were all at a loss.

Rick said, "Well, since this hasn't gotten us anywhere, what if we meet again tomorrow afternoon at Hyde's Peak Beach and do a little reconnaissance work? We could make a driftwood fort to serve as a blind, and then spy on the water fowl that live there. If we don't spot any clues, no loss. We can just hang out."

I have to admit, sometimes Rick has great ideas – for a little brother, that is.

II

AT THE SEASIDE the next day, our lovable canine Billy was running around as only he can – in and out of the sparse beach traffic, sand flying, projecting spit and generally wreaking havoc, when he stopped abruptly and snatched something from the sand – something he obviously coveted. We gave chase for the sheer fun of it before we realized what his prized booty was.

"Guys, wait. Billy! Come here, boy. Come on." I didn't know what he had exactly, but from the fleeting glimpse I got, I thought it might be something special. I needed to get it before it became pup-meal. "Billy, come on." That dog! Although we'd spent heaps of time training him, apparently little of it had taken. I figured he might just have to get by on his looks.

Wrestling Billy to the ground, we managed to extract the now dripping treasure from his mouth. It was the smooth, skeletal remains of a sand dollar – or sand-cake, pansy shell or cake-urchin, if you will – a flat, burrowing sea urchin that's shaped like a large, fuzzy (when alive) cookie, but this was unlike any I'd ever seen before. It was gold. Most sand dollars are a tanned, sandy colour but when they die (and are more readily found on a beach) the outer shell becomes a sun-bleached white. Only this one was undeniably iridescent amber. It's almost mystical floral pore markings gleamed.

"I don't believe this, another mystery to solve! What's going on around here?" Jerry was evidently perplexed and I know he's not a great fan of that feeling. He usually has a pretty good grasp on things.

"Hey! Look at this!" called Rick. He had moved off to investigate the surrounding area, apparently searching for clues. "It's a whole bunch of them."

We nearly knocked him over in our haste to reach his side. "What?" I looked down to see what the sand offered. "Did you find them like this or did you arrange them in this ring?" I couldn't quite believe what I was seeing. Not just one fantastic glistening, golden sand dollar. Seven of them. Placed in a perfectly round circle – so evenly spaced, it looked like it was mathematically exact.

"I found them like this and look what else I found".

Rick walked a few paces from us, bent down and held something aloft. Another amazing golden feather.

"No way! Get out!" Something very bizarre was going on.

I gave my head a purposeful shake "Guys. I don't know about you, but this has all the makings of driving me a little nutty. Don't say it, Rick! These things just don't seem natural. Do you think someone is playing a prank on us?" I looked around expectantly. The thought had never occurred to me until I started speaking. That happens to me sometimes.

Conversely, Rita exuded composure. "Let's build that fort Rick suggested. I think a little covert operation might be in order." Rita and Rick set off immediately to gather the requisite driftwood building materials leaving Jerry and me to consider what had just unfolded.

"Alex, what do you make of all this?"

"Dunno. But I really hope that I'm ready for it, whatever *it* is."

III

IT'S FUNNY, BUT at the time, about the most exciting thing that had ever happened to Rick and me revolved around losing our luggage at the Vancouver airport. Now that was an adventure! Yet these findings, the golden feathers and sand dollars, led us to places we never could have dreamt. I'll get to the details shortly, but for now, you'll just have to be patient. And read carefully. You don't want to miss anything. Oh, and just so you know, my dictionary and I are very close – I learn a new word every day. So please forgive a little compulsive polysyllabic vocabularizing now and then – oh, sorry – there I go again!

Yes, we set up that driftwood fort for our undercover work and pretty much inhabited it daily for a few days. We were ever hopeful of spotting something – anything – that would help unravel this mystery. And when we finally witnessed something of interest, we were ready. Well...sort of.

"Wait." Rita went stock-still. "Listen."

"What is it?"

"Shhh!"

Then I heard it too. Seeming to seep through that misty Sunday morning fog in late September was a persistent hum as high-pitched as you'll ever hear. Yet though it was high-pitched, at the same time it was oddly soothing. It grew, filling up the empty space of the day's grey heaviness. It seemed to be emanating from the ocean – a longing, haunting resonance but with a suggestion of some kind of invisible tow. Almost magnetic.

As we listened, spellbound, the mist's veil began to thin, revealing more of the steel blue sea and somehow the sound became increasingly clear – more distinct. Finally, something moved lazily out of the film of vapour.

"Look! It's a swan," I yelled out, blundering, caught up in the moment and shattering the enchantment. And at that moment, the extraordinary, sweeping notes ceased. Only the sounds of gently lapping waves remained.

The swan, visibly startled by my outburst, stopped its approach but lingered, gazing at us rapt, lightly bobbing with the swells.

Rita sighed, "It's magnificent." It had very much the typical, everyday splendour of any elegant, so-white-it's-almost-prismatic, swan but it seemed to glisten slightly even in the overcast gloom.

"Rita," I murmured, "let's try to get closer." The two of us left the fort warily, mindful that any abrupt movement might break what remained of the already fractured spell. The swan eyed us suspiciously and then astonishingly, moved closer – as if it were as curious about us as we were of it.

Why we didn't leave that dog at home, I'll never know. But suddenly, man, out he hurtled, riotously barking at the swan as only a bungling Golden Retriever can. Generally, no one takes him very seriously, but unfortunately, that swan decided to.

While the boys attempted to rein in the wannabe ruffian, Rita and I tried to coax the swan to remain but she circled neatly and moved back into the fog, melting away from view as though she'd never been.

I turned to Billy and said, "Thanks," in my best 'not impressed' tone. He looked up at me lovingly, tongue lolling nearly to the sand, proud of his ferocious (not) display – naive to the damage he'd left in his wake. Okay, I caved. I forgave him with a shake of my head and a chuckle, and mussed the top of his fluffy, befuddled head.

Getting back to the swan business, Rita exclaimed, "That was remarkable!"

"And peculiar." I added.

"It *was* bizarre how the swan came out of the fog like that. And that weird tone...it only stopped when Alex yelled."

"But really, what do you think that sound was? What could have made a noise like that?"

"I know that sometimes sound seems to travel differently through a fog. It was a strange frequency..." Jerry stops. He appeared to be considering possible theories. He knows a lot about electronics, frequencies, science. He's really handy to have around.

"I think the swan was that alien bird I was talking about when this whole thing started."

"Rick!" Rita, Jerry and I were used to Rick's imagination running wild and his love of all things fantastic, but this was too much – or was he on to something? I gulped, thought about it, gulped again. No. It couldn't be...could it?

As we walked home through the now-lifting fog, we discussed our next course of action.

"When we get home I am going to do another Internet search – this time on swans, music in the mist, golden sand dollars and feathers – everything I can think of and see what comes up. There must be something out there. And, I'll even consider some of the more far-fetched explanations." I looked pointedly at Rick.

"It's about time. I was wondering when you were going to come over to the dark side. HAHAHA!" – a mock diabolical laugh. My brother is quite the piece of work. I wonder where he gets it.

While the others enthusiastically voiced their protests, I moved to the edge of the melee and surrendered to my thoughts. Something had struck me when I considered the list of potential search engine words. A sketchy outline of an admittedly fantastic theory began to take shape at that moment. "Wait. Hold on you guys..." Was I being too hasty? "It's probably nothing...certainly crazy..."

"What, Alex? What is it?"

"Well..." I was reluctant to leave the safety of my ledge but I thought that since I was among friends, what could happen? I hurled myself into the abyss. "Golden feathers, an alluring song in the mist, a swan...There's a myth – Slavic, I think – that involves a *Wila*, a kind of nymph that lives by or in the ocean. She can shape-shift into all kinds of animals and birds and she lures people with her song – kind of like a Siren. It's in a book I read on myths of the world that my mom bought me."

"Oh yeah. I read about Sirens in *The Odyssey*." Jerry said.

Rick burst in. "Alex, you're not saying what I think you're saying, are you? I mean, it's kind of ridiculous, isn't it?"

I couldn't believe it. My brother had actually found a limit to what he would accept. He asked again, "This couldn't possibly happen, could it, Alex?" Then he looked at me with a mix of alarm and pleading.

We all fell silent.

Finally, Jerry burst through any private ruminations. "No. This is ludicrous, impossible. Surely it's just a myth. There must be some other explanation..."

"I don't know," I replied. I decided right then and there that I wouldn't commit to any theory without further investigation. "First things, first. The Internet."

IV

"WELL," I SIGHED. "That was both informative and...disconcerting."

To sum it up, according to Slavic mythology, not only can *Wilas* shape-shift into all kinds of animals and sing to lure people to them, they have absolute power over the weather and are fierce warriors. Great.

After Rita, Jerry and Rick had reflected on the information we had gathered, they all came to the same sweeping verdict about the *Wila* link to our beach cache: "It's crazy! Ridiculous! Outrageous!" You get the point. But sadly for me, I simply couldn't move past that nagging uncertainty that droned in the back of my brain, dulling all rational thought.

I was determined to settle the matter (probably more for myself than anyone else) one way or another, once and for all, come what may. I offered a plan that I am sure frustrated the others but brought me some semblance of peace of mind. "Okay, you guys. This is what I propose. Rick and I are heading to the library tomorrow with Mom. Tonight I'll do a library search on the net and hopefully put some books on hold that will provide more information on *Wilas*, sand dollars, golden feathers, whatever." Then, noting their looks of bafflement, I added, "Don't get me wrong. I'm not convinced about this *Wila* thing either but maybe with more research I can finally rule it out completely and move on. And, who knows, maybe all this research will lead to a breakthrough."

I continued, "Rita and Jerry, how about if you look over what material you have at home? You must have some books on mythology and natural sciences lying around. Come on, guys. Maybe you have something that can help shed some light on all this. Let's meet again on Wednesday – say, two o'clock – to talk about what we find out. Okay?"

Rick interjected, "Sorry, Alex. You forget. We've got swimming lessons on Wednesdays. Life goes on, you know. Let's make it Thursday." He looked to Rita and Jerry for consent. They nodded agreeably.

And I smiled, relieved. Apparently my hair-splitting was fair to middling.

V

THURSDAY DELIVERED THE four of us as planned, back to Hyde's Peak Beach, but all discussions of *Wilas* were promptly shelved. Our esteemed hangout, the driftwood fort, had been pummelled. Substantial logs littered the area as if they were little more than discarded lawn clippings. A violent storm had struck Wednesday night leaving a desolated coastline in its wake. In dismay, we set to work reassembling what we could of our lookout when, from behind, someone spoke.

"Want a hand?"

Gaping at each other in turn, we slowly twisted around to spy who this oddly-timbred, raspy voice belonged to.

She was dressed all in black. A punk rock kind of girl. About sixteen. Spiky, close-cropped, severely frosted pink hair, ripped jeans, an assortment of safety pins in inspired places – you know the type. But what set her apart (other than her voice, of course) was her face.

Now, as you know, I'm 12. I'll admit, I'm starting to pay a bit more attention to my appearance. I brush my hair every day – without being asked, if you can imagine. I bathe regularly. Yes, really. As for my face, well, it's a regular kind of face, I guess. I don't know… I have noticed that it has a natural, outdoorsy kind of colour to it and I've unfortunately had the occasional zit – gross. What was interesting about this girl was that her skin seemed to…well…have a light behind it. It seemed to glow – in a pale, translucent, flawless, aberrant, vampire kind of way. What was that all about, anyway?

"Oh, hi, we didn't see you there."

No. She wasn't what you would call conventionally beautiful or anything, but she was definitely, shall we say...distinctive. I took a sidelong glance at Jerry and noted a heightened colour rising in his face.

"Would you like some help? I guess your fort went down in the storm last night."

There's that accent again. Maybe not an accent so much as variations in sound attributed to a physical feature perhaps.

"Sure, I guess," Rick said. I was glad that someone else had finally found their tongue.

At that, she lifted a nearby log that would have taxed a much larger person. We watched her shyly as she carefully positioned it just so.

"I'm Alex. This is my brother Rick and our friends Rita and Jerry," I said, gesturing to no one in particular as I said their names.

She paused in her work. "I'm Olesia. Just call me Lessie."

"Are you from around here, Lessie?" Rita asked hesitantly.

"Well, I am now."

We worked in a kind of charged silence for a while, starkly conscious of each other's movements, keeping our distance, but eventually I think we all relaxed into private daydreams. Finally, Lessie broke our musings with, "So, why aren't you guys in school?"

We stopped to meet each other's eyes, the four of us grinning slightly in the shared experience. This question always comes up. I decided to offer my practised response. "We're homeschooled.

We tend to do our school work in the mornings or evenings so we have most afternoons free."

"Oh, I see." She appeared to be thinking this through and then declared, "How about if I told you that no one goes to school?"

What was this all about? Guardedly I answered, anxiously trying to gauge where this could possibly be headed, "Of course people go to school. You know, most kids go to school. We have many friends that go to school."

Lessie considered me for an instant then offered the following challenge. "But, what if I told you that I can prove it?"

The four of us looked at each other in bewilderment. What was she talking about?

Finally, "Okay. I'll bite. Prove it," Jerry faced her squarely.

Seeming to take a moment to compose herself, Lessie began, "Well, let's say a normal school year runs about 180 days. There are 365 days in a year, right? You can subtract a third of those days because of sleep. So that leaves..."

"243." Rick was always a math whiz kid.

"Right. 243 days. And you have to eat. So let's take off three hours per day for meals. So that leaves..."

This took a little more time. "243 minus 30 days equal 213 days." Thanks, Rick.

"Okay, 213 days left. Do you want Christmas, spring break and summer vacations? Take off another 75 days or so for them and that leaves 138 days. And we haven't even taken into account statutory holidays, Saturdays and Sundays! So, no one goes to school. There's no time."

My lower jaw dropped. "Wait! What? How'd you do that?"

She laughed. A chiming kind of laugh.

Rick sounded only a tad confident when he said, "I don't know how you did that but I'm going to figure it out."

"Okay. You know, it's getting kind of late. Let's meet here tomorrow afternoon and you can enlighten us. Deal?" Lessie said, moving away almost imperceptibly.

"Okay. I'll figure this out, you know." Rick set his jaw and I smiled to myself. I knew it would be a quiet walk home.

We left Lessie at the beach, singing our goodbyes and began a slow walk home. Naturally, Rick strayed behind in obvious mathematical delight, gesturing now and then, mumbling to himself. Jerry, Rita and I took this opportunity to discuss the day's events and our new friend – if that is indeed what she was. I wasn't certain.

Lessie was nice enough in a retro, unconventional, atypical kind of way. But something about her was unsettling. It was like there was some sort of weird barrier separating her from the rest of us. She only allowed us to get marginally close to her physically and, it seemed, even emotionally for that matter. But, hey, what the heck! It was only the first time we'd met and she *had* invited us to meet with her again the next day.

Of course, Rita said, "I like her." There were few people Rita didn't like.

"I'm not sure what to make of her. I liked her riddle though." Typical Jerry. Just the facts.

When we arrived home, Rick, with pencil and paper in hand, marched up to his room and promptly closed his door. He clearly felt compelled to solve Lessie's riddle. We still hadn't been able to outright discard the possible relationship between a *Wila* and our beach spoils so I opted to re-examine the stack of library books that I had commandeered from the local library. No rest for the obsessed, I guess!

VI

"HEY GUYS! OVER here." It was Lessie. It appeared that she'd been waiting for us. In one arm, weighing her down slightly, was an intricately woven picnic basket. I eyed it hopefully.

"I'm glad you made it. I thought it would be nice if we had a little picnic." She led us to the back of our fort (happily still standing) where a teal, black and gold blanket covered in a pattern of zigzag scallops had been carefully laid out on the sand between haphazardly placed driftwood planks. She proceeded to unpack an aromatic selection of round honey cakes, a variety of fresh fruits and vegetables, lemonade...

"Wow this is amazing! You can invite us to our fort anytime," said Jerry, tucking in.

"I just thought it would be nice to share this with you. I had a good time yesterday..." I barely heard her as we followed Jerry's lead, smacking lips, slurping lemonade. After a considerable length of time (we were apparently hungry), conversation resumed when Lessie asked, "So, Rick, did you figure out that riddle?"

"As a matter of fact, I did," said Rick. At least I think that's what he said. It was a bit of a muffled response given the sizable bite of honey cake he was still chewing. We waited for him to finish but, to be honest, I don't think any one of us was especially interested in this Math problem, considering such luscious cakes were still in the vicinity.

Finally, he continued. "Okay, here goes." He cleared his throat. "You should have simply subtracted the vacation days and weekends from 365. But, by taking off the time spent eating and sleeping, you were in effect double dipping – eating and sleeping happen during vacations times too – and that's how you ran out of days," he said, dipping a carrot into some delectable spinach dip.

Lessie smiled and said, "You got it! I'm so glad." The rest of us applauded and despite Rick being my nemesis half the time, I found myself cheering the loudest. Lessie continued, "Telling riddles and doing puzzles are favourite pastimes in my circle."

As we continued our out-and-out feast, Lessie chatted amicably and we were able to learn a few more things about her like...the hair dye she used is called Pink Pearl, her favourite seafood is Dungeness crab and the leather pouch she wears around her neck is called a *ladanki*.

Sated, we migrated to the surrounding area to instinctively begin a session of beach combing (I was ever-watchful for supernatural oddities) and impromptu rock climbing along the boulder-rich shore. As the daylight began to ebb, we thanked Lessie for the fabulous banquet and travelled back to our respective homes. As we ambled along the well-used forest path, we discussed the events of the day and our latest impressions of Lessie.

"She's great!" Naturally, this praise came from Rita. But this time she seemed less-than-convinced, for she continued with,

"But you guys were right. She can be a little peculiar at times...Like, we have no idea where she lives, where she's from, or what she does when we're not there. I mean, she's a bit evasive."

"Yeah. I know. And what's with the *ladanki*. The punk look – okay. We all need to express ourselves, but didn't you think that pouch-like thing didn't quite go with the punk rock get-up?" Jerry can be so suspicious at times. I knew I'd seen a thing like that *ladanki* before somewhere. It wasn't *so* strange and besides, Lessie had every right to wear what she wanted to wear.

"Well," I pitched in. "I like her. Oh! And by the way...we've got to talk about our seaside mystery. Rick and I haven't really uncovered anything that we can use to discount a *Wila* correlation with the beach paraphernalia – but we're still looking. How about you guys? Got any leads?"

"No, not a thing. But I was thinking..." Jerry seemed to be reflecting on something. "Maybe we should just be more vigilant when we're at the beach and really keep our eyes open." He then added, "More clues could be out there waiting for us and we would never know – Lessie's been a huge distraction these last couple days."

"And that's what I wanted to talk to you about. I think that maybe, if you all agree, we should let Lessie in on our mysterious finds. And our theory about the *Wila*. I think she might be able to give us a fresh perspective. She seems to know a lot of stuff. "

"I don't think that's a good idea, Alex." That was Rita – yes, Rita – the one who's forever upbeat and generous and yet...quite intuitive at times.

"Why not, Rita?" asked Rick, who'd been occupying the outskirts of our circle until now. "I mean, she seems to want to be our friend."

"I don't know. I just have a feeling we should wait until we know her a bit better before we let her in on the mystery and all our weird theories. Who knows what she'd even think?"

"Okay, fair enough. We won't say anything to Lessie. Besides, Rick and I won't see you guys for a couple of days. Mom and Dad want us to go to the seminars on global warming at the university tomorrow. I'll give you guys a shout next week."

VII

LIKE EVERY OTHER kid out there inhabiting this 21st century, I know plenty about global warming, but these lectures at the university turned out to be really enlightening. Like, did you know that the world's oceans absorb carbon dioxide just like the atmosphere does? And that they are getting more acidic because of it? That the oceans are also getting warmer and this contributes to more violent storms? I watch the news sometimes with my mom and dad and I have to say, there certainly seem to have been a lot more hurricanes and monster storms happening over the last few years. I sure hope that whatever is going on out there can be reversed because these freak storms are beginning to well...yes...freak me out.

I called Rita and told her all about the lectures. She was really interested in what I had to report. We speculated about how we could do our part for the environment and we arranged to visit the library on Friday night to get more ideas. We also made plans to wake up bright and early Saturday morning to head to the beach with the boys.

VIII

WE WALKED OUR way through another heavy, soaking fog. We couldn't see that far ahead of us but we certainly knew our way well enough. Just ahead lay our destination.

Hyde's Peak is a rocky, yet still tree-bearing outcrop on the northeast arm of the beach and regional park that bear its name. It's kind of a desolate place up there – windswept conifers lean bent by the relentless wind and what grass manages to survive on its rocky edge is sand-pelted. Arbutus trees form a grove on the bluff and extend almost to the ocean's shore. They look like gnarled fingers grasping sea spray. The pungent smell of the ocean completes the ambiance.

The beach, with its rock-strewn, tree-heavy landscape is a great place to hang out. There's no mistaking it. It's not tranquil, mile on mile white sand, stick your umbrella in the ground and enjoy. Oh no. It's not for the uninitiated. It's a wild place of intense natural beauty and it's ripe with incalculable possibilities. Interesting formations and hidden alcoves provide a backdrop to this beach that has fuelled many of our days with fun and wonder. This is why we were so incensed by what we found there that Saturday morning.

"Oh no! Look what someone did." Rick said with disgust. We caught up with him and gathered around the crime scene. For a minute, no one could even speak.

Rita's voice quaked. "Why would someone do this?" It was her favourite arbutus tree. It had stood at least 50 feet tall, branching out in its red barked, broad-leafed splendour. It had been deliberately chopped down and left to rot. Its limbs lay in a dishevelled heap, unwanted. The remaining stump was stark as a bleeding, inflamed sore.

We quickly studied the area to see if there were any other casualties. No, it seemed this was the only fatality.

We hadn't been up here for a few days. Preoccupation with various homeschooling projects had grabbed all our attention that week. "I wonder when this happened," Jerry said.

"I think it's recent." Remnants of the axe's work were strewn haphazardly and appeared to be freshly wrought.

"This just feels like such a violation." Rita was not the only one to feel the sting of grief. I too was having a hard time fathoming this dishonourable act and it left me feeling sullied.

Rick asked, "What should we do?"

There was not much we could do besides report it to the city officials. The damage was done, but perhaps by reporting it, we could prevent such a thing from happening again.

We moved further into the arbutus grove, carefully re-examining each tree that we passed, fearful of discovering further damage when Rick cried out in surprise. I then witnessed something that derailed my focus.

About 25 feet off the forest floor, on the north side of a wonderfully peeling, orange trunked arbutus tree, was what looked like a notebook sized, white-washed front door trimmed in moss green. A coffee-coloured lion's head knocker functioned as its only adornment – no door knob could be seen from our vantage point.

"It's so cute! I wish we could get up there," Rita exclaimed.

"I wonder who put that there. It's so whimsical." I thought it was a really neat thing to do.

The door's quirky 'magic' was lost on the boys. "Come on. Let's keep going. I don't know why somebody would put that up there. I just want to finish checking the rest of the grove."

"Ah, Jerry. Why is it that you can entertain the existence of a *Wila* but a fairy is way too out there for you?" I teased as we followed his lead through the forest.

Not long after this interlude, Billy caught sight of something he just had to investigate. We ended our own quest to once again chase after that darn dog.

IX

OCTOBER STALKED OFF laying waste with frequent downpours and the occasional wind storm. We met up with Lessie nearly every week or so and managed to establish an amiable if limited friendship with her. It didn't sit well with me that we spent so much time with her but still didn't let her in on the *Wila* issue.

I think we were all pretty preoccupied with the search for new clues, but Lessie didn't seem to notice. That could be because we hadn't seen much to get keyed up about. We did manage to find one more golden sand dollar though, which Rick pocketed swiftly as soon as he found it, but that was about it. Any discussion on the topic of *Wilas* was reserved for when we left Lessie alone at the beach and began our walks home.

One weekday morning in early November, my Mom needed to run into town for an appointment. On hearing this, I called Jerry and Rita and got them to convince their mom to forgo their homeschooling routine until later so we could all take advantage of a sunny morning.

"We don't see the sun much in winter, Mom. We need our vitamin D."

It worked. Within 20 minutes, Rick and I picked up Rita and Jerry at their house to spend a few stolen hours at the beach.

It felt like we had seen nothing but dreary grey for weeks on end. It was a sparklingly fresh day, so bright you swear you saw spots.

Upon arriving at the beach, I shielded my eyes against the sun-reflecting glare of the ocean. I gazed down from a raised bank and spotted Lessie, a solitary figure on the deserted beach. It was strange though. She was moving about – dancing airily along the sand but not really dancing – more like gliding in circles. She obviously hadn't noticed us. I motioned to the others to stop and pointed in her direction. Rick was about to call out to her when Lessie began to revolve on the spot, faster and faster. I wanted to somehow reach out to her but what I was witnessing was too disturbing for that. She was spinning so rapidly she actually started to blur and then, to my horror, her image appeared to melt into a kind of barren vortex. Just when she had almost completely disappeared, a bird – a white bird – a falcon, rose from where she'd just been spinning, taking what remained of her likeness with it, as it launched itself skyward in the direction of Hyde's Peak.

A scream rose from beside me. It was Rita, panic-stricken. Jerry and Rick both shouted and raced along the beach toward the spot where Lessie had last stood. I was mute, too traumatized to react. I felt someone grip my hand and before I knew what was happening, I was dragged toward the scene of Lessie's undoing.

Rita and I reached the site just as Rick snatched an object from the sand. It was a golden sand dollar, one of seven, all in a meticulous ring, precisely where Lessie had danced.

Jerry was the first to muster a coherent sentence. Gesturing, he said, "The bird flew over there. Let's see if we can find it."

Our only response was to move silently, tracking the prints he set down in the sand one by one, away from the ring of sand dollars and our established reality.

I think Rita knew instinctively just where to look. She briskly took the lead from Jerry and led us toward the rocky shoreline and past the downed arbutus tree. Following the rough pathway between matronly spires, we meandered until we came to the arbutus which housed the curious fairy door. With brutal dignity, sitting on an adjacent limb, was a pure white falcon. We gazed helplessly in its direction.

"I heard you scream." The voice was unmistakably Lessie's but my mind was having trouble accepting what I was seeing.

Apparently sensing our unease, the falcon lifted gracefully from its perch and glided down to land on the soft forest floor in front of us. Silently, it began to jump in and out of focus until it shape-shifted violently to once again reveal our friend. Her face appeared unmoved, but she was betrayed by the single tear that escaped her guarded eyes. We stood staring at her, unable to fashion a single word. Lessie broke the impasse.

"I think you know what I am."

Silence.

"Please say something. I..." she broke off, evidently unable to continue.

"Are you a *Wila*?" Jerry had moved forward bravely.

"I'm known by many names. *Wila, Willi, Veela*. I am a type of nymph."

"Lessie, what...Are you all alone or are there many of you?" I was proud of Rick. I still wasn't able to speak.

"I am the only one in this area, but we can be found all over the world."

Rita joined in, "Why didn't you tell us? I thought we were friends?"

Lessie's poise seemed to diminish slightly as she said, without meeting anyone's eyes, "I guess I was afraid of how you would react. I liked all of you the moment I spied you, well...spying on me."

My courage came with my indignation, "What do you mean 'spying on you'? We never spied on you."

"Well, yes, you did. I was the swan you saw that day."

This was too much. "Lessie, you should have told us from the start. We had a right to know. You were our friend." Rita was visibly upset.

Lessie countered, "You could have let me in on your mystery items. You could have shared your ideas with me. It could have been so different. I was afraid..."

She had a point, but we were well beyond that.

Rita said, "I think we better go." She backed away briskly and grabbed my hand. She led me without speaking back through the trees of Hyde's Peak, back toward the beach.

Jerry and Rick followed our lead. I looked back in time to witness Lessie's upturned chin tremble but refuse to drop.

It took time, but during that cheerless walk from the beach, I realized that I wasn't at all happy the way we had left things with Lessie, but I truly couldn't think much beyond that. Not one of us spoke until we stumbled up to Jerry's and Rita's front door.

"Well...mystery solved. Now what?" My hollow attempt at lightening the mood fell utterly flat.

Jerry's natural composure brought me some relief, "I suppose time will help. Go home, you guys. Let's clear our heads and sleep on this. Hopefully we'll see things more clearly tomorrow."

X

THAT NIGHT, RICK and I feigned fatigue and went to bed early. I think we both felt the need to distance ourselves from any troubling thoughts associated with the events that had happened earlier that day. You know, sleep will often present a welcome respite for a burdened mind. As I lay in bed willing slumber to perform its charm, wouldn't you know it, a low rumble shook the house, like the shudder made if a giant, a mile away, were to smash the ground with his fist. The house stilled directly and then trembled once more, as if to stress the point.

Rick came rushing into my room. "Did you feel that? Was it an earthquake?"

"Yeah, I think it was." We yelled down to Mom and Dad and they confirmed it.

"Everything is okay. Try to get back to sleep," Mom called.

Now, unless you live in an earthquake zone like us, this almost matter-of-fact exchange may seem bizarre. But we're accustomed to these minor rumblings. Most of the time, fortunately, there is no damage and life goes on without a blip on the radar. We've been spared...so far. We all know that a big one is coming, but no one really knows when. For all we know, it could be 300 years away. Or tomorrow. In the meantime, all we can really do is make sure that we have our earthquake preparedness kit ready and periodically go through a drill – much like an annual fire drill. After that, you just have to live your life. Right?

XI

RICK AND I did finally manage to settle down enough that night to give way to forty or so winks. However, for me, vivid dreams of violent storms and harrowing shipwrecks ruled my night-time siesta. When at long last morning arrived, I felt far from rested but was relieved to escape my dramatic, zonked-out ordeal. I stretched and made a reluctant glance outside. Rain. So what else is new? And then, like an embalmer's winding sheet blackening the day, I recalled the events of the previous morning and how we had behaved toward Lessie. As the full weight of it crashed in around me, I felt dreadful. We had to fix this.

I tossed my bedding aside, threw my legs hastily over the side of my bed and made tracks to Rick's room. He was already awake, but just lying there, staring at the ceiling. He turned to look at me, sluggish. His eyes spoke of his deep regret and I knew in that moment, it was settled – he was as committed to mending our relationship with Lessie as I was.

That afternoon, Rick and I walked decisively to Jerry's and Rita's house.

As soon as we were settled snugly beside their warm fire, I began. "I don't know about you guys, but Rick and I feel terrible about how we treated Lessie."

Rita sat quietly. She was pale and appeared to be having trouble meeting my gaze.

"Rita, are you okay?" I asked.

"I...I couldn't sleep last night."

"I know. It must have taken me an hour or so after the earthquake hit to--yeah, guys, did you feel it last night?"

"Yeah, we did. No damage or anything. Just shook the house," Jerry said.

"So anyway," said Rick, getting back on topic, "what are we going to do about Lessie?"

Rita shifted uncomfortably. Fortunately, her always-earnest brother, Jerry was on the same page as Rick and I.

"It's obvious. We need to make it up to Lessie. Yes, she kept something really big from us, but can we honestly say that we would have behaved any differently if it was one of us who had such a huge, unbelievable secret? I mean, come on. Bottom line is she's our friend. We can move past this. Can't we?"

Rita, at long last, found her voice. "I don't know if I can, but I think we need to try."

That was all we needed to hear. We gathered our jackets, slipped on our boots and made for the door.

XII

THE SKY HAD darkened threateningly. The rain was falling much more heavily. Looking back, I'm convinced there must have been a flood watch in effect, but at the time, we were pretty much oblivious to the deluge.

We entered the arbutus grove from the north side, tense but determined. The trees offered negligible shelter from the downpour. We trudged on, ducking the low hanging branches until, over the beating rhythm of the rain, we heard...cursing. We stopped to confirm what we were hearing and then as one, we raced toward the litany. It was Lessie...in obvious trouble. When we reached her, what we found made us instantly catch our breath.

Lessie's arbutus tree had been ripped violently from the ground. Its roots reached ten feet skyward exposing a filthy yawning chasm. We catapulted to where her white door should have been but all that remained was a small mass of splintered wood hanging by a single bent nail. The lion's head knocker was nowhere in sight. White feathers littered the surrounding area.

"Lessie!" I screamed. "Lessie, where are you?" We struggled, frantically trying to pinpoint the spot her voice radiated from. At length, her cursing stopped. She had evidently heard our shouts for she called, "I'm here. I'm trapped inside the tree." It was plain that she was trying to sound calm.

"Lessie, are you okay? There are white feathers strewn everywhere..." As if on cue, Rick began to gather them in fistfuls. I'm sure he was as desperate as the rest of us to put things right.

"Yeah, I'm not hurt, but I can't get out of here. It's a spell..." She hesitated. "What are you guys doing here?"

I hurtled forward, "Lessie, we're so sorry about yesterday. I guess we were just shocked by the whole *Wila* thing and forgot about what your friendship really means to us."

Jerry was impatient. "A spell? Lessie, who did this to you?" He was busy inspecting the space her door once occupied.

"It was Gwidon. He's a *Vodianoi* – a kind of water spirit. He was ruthless! I've never seen him like this before. He's kind of a miserable guy to be around even on a good day but he usually just avoids others. And he's certainly not usually one to be so violent. Did you guys feel it?"

"Feel what?" I asked.

"Oh, you probably thought it was just an earthquake. He was so furious last night that he actually caused the ground to shake, right before he singlehandedly uprooted my arbutus tree."

I felt struck dumb. Unaware, I began to wring my hands. This was just too much to take in all at once.

Somehow Rita managed to quell her emotions. In a calm-sounding voice she asked, "Why did he do this to you?" Her face revealed nothing. She looked stoical.

Lessie hesitated. "I'm not really sure. All I know is that he was after one of my golden feathers. You see, while I'm a swan, if one of my golden feathers is plucked from me – the ones at the tip of my wings – the bearer gains power over the weather. You know, storms and stuff. Beyond that, I have no idea what he could possibly be after...he was really out of control." And at that, as if the enormity of the situation had finally taken hold, Lessie began to cry. She made little mewling sounds that were barely discernible above the clamour of the rain.

"Lessie, please don't," soothed Rick. "We'll get you out of there. We'll think of something," but he sounded more desperate than he probably would have liked.

Between sobs, Lessie asked, "What do you care, really? After all that's happened, why would you want anything to do with a *Wila*?" She practically spat the final word.

I rushed to speak. "Lessie, you cannot know how sorry we are." I bent over the log trying to get closer to her. "We should have remembered that you were our friend and cut you a bit of slack. It couldn't have been easy for you to keep your secret. I'm sure you wanted to tell us, but you were probably unsure about how we'd react. And as it turned out, you were right to be apprehensive. Look at how badly we behaved when we did find out." By this time, I was pleading. "Lessie, please accept our apology. And please let us help you."

After what seemed like a generation, just audible through the rain we heard Lessie say, "I could have handled it all differently too. Yes, I forgive you."

Rick could never handle too much touchy-feely stuff. "Enough of this peace and love stuff! What's our next step?"

Lessie answered somewhat breathlessly, "Please listen closely. I haven't got much time left. Soon you won't be able to hear me. I will be too far gone within the tree. Here is what you need to do to stop him from destroying the world."

I gulped. Did she say what I thought she said? What the heck were we getting ourselves into? Would the *Vodianoi*, this Gwidon, really be able to do that? Since freaking out has never gotten me anywhere, I decided that the best thing for me to do was to try to remain calm.

She continued, "With the power he has gained from my golden feather, he will be able to create the worst storms imaginable, storms that are capable of forever altering the planet. Oh yeah. And he knows all about you. He's been watching us from somewhere off the beach."

She paused as if to let this soak in, then went on. "Over the next while he is going to play an ugly game with you. Every week or so he will return to this spot with a riddle that you must solve before seven days are up. There will be four riddles in total, each more challenging than the last. And it is only when you solve each and every one of these riddles that you will be able to stop him from totally destroying the world."

It was getting increasingly hard to hear her but she persisted, "The storms will grow in intensity after each week and will only end with the successful unravelling of the final riddle. He has already started this terrible game. This downpour is his doing". Her voice faded off like it was entering a void. As if by some covert signal, lightning flashed across the sky.

"Lessie," Jerry shouted above the insistent downpour. "I need to get this straight.. If we solve all these riddles not only will Gwidon stop the storms, he will set you free, right?"

Try as we might, we could not hear her response. But as if to close the deal, lightning flashed once more, raking the sky like so many gnarled, ghoulish fingers.

"Lessie?"

Still nothing.

I began to cry, but no one noticed. My tears mixed with the unrelenting raindrops that soaked my face.

XIII

THAT CRUEL RAINFALL drenched us completely but it wasn't until Rick and I finally arrived home that we even noticed it. In complete silence, we staggered to our respective bedrooms to change our sodden clothes.

After struggling into a warm sweater and jeans, I gazed out my bedroom window, feeling numbed by the experience, equally blind to the torrential downpour outside. Unceasing rivulets ran down our driveway but my mind was only open to thoughts of Lessie. Our friend. Could we save our friend? And would it really be up to us to save the world? This burden weighed on me and I was scared. What were we going to do? Would we be able to face this evil *Vodianoi*, let along solve the mysterious riddles? Breaking through my anguished thoughts was the sound of my mom, asking for "a little help setting the table, please." Even with the weight of the world on our shoulders, it apparently continued to spin.

Later that evening, Jerry called. Rick was still too shaken, so I answered. We made plans to meet the next afternoon at the beach.

XIV

A FIGURE BECKONED to us. It was Jerry. He looked rested and exuded a poised, self-assurance I'd never seen before. Gone was any trace of the unsteadiness of the previous day. My demeanour must have played in marked contrast. I hadn't slept well, had bags under my eyes that no cucumber could combat, and I was in a decidedly vulnerable state. Not at all my all-powerful, capable self. And the foul weather didn't help matters any.

"Hi," I mumbled. Rick stayed back. He hadn't fared much better last night. In many ways, it's often my state of mind that dictates how Rick will react to a situation – although I'm sure he'd never admit that.

Jerry launched in with, "Rita and I have been talking and we're confident that we can get through this." It is funny how different two families can be.

We've known Jerry and Rita pretty much our entire lives. We have about a billion pictures of them in our photo albums in various situations throughout the years – birthdays, Christmas, Easter, summer holidays, Halloween, assorted homeschooling projects, just hanging out. We get along really well with their parents too. I would say Rick and I are really lucky because you could say we almost have two families. But man, are those two families like chalk and cheese.

What can I say about my parents? Well, first there's my mom. She takes her job as a homeschooling parent pretty seriously but she's a lot of fun, too. I would say she is both our mom and our friend. Dad keeps us laughing and he's really smart – in a totally awesome way. He's an IT consultant and a musician – quite the combination. And with him around, there's never a dull moment. But what defines our family is that while in many ways we live a typical, white-picket-fence kind of conventional life most of the time, we reserve a lot of time for fun. Things that are daring, outside of the box or that exhibit a bit of an edge appeal to us. Show us a happy accident by Marcel Duchamp and we totally get it.

Jerry's and Rita's family is pretty much the exact opposite. But don't get me wrong. They're a pretty traditional family too, but their ideas of fun and ours are poles apart. Whereas we revel in the spontaneous and ground-breaking, they rejoice in the planned and time-honoured – but in a wonderfully mellow way. I guess you could say that they're classical music to our rock 'n' roll. Our glue is our respect for our differences and our harmonizing lifestyles. We complement each other really well and I must say, having two houses you can seriously call home is a great way to grow up.

So it's my awareness of these basic differences between the two families that really made Rita's and Jerry's apparent composure extraordinary. And here I'd thought Rick and I were the plucky ones.

When we looked at them like they had kangaroos coming out of their ears, Rita added, "No guys, really. We can do this. One step at a time." Although her words sounded confident, I could sense an underlying uneasiness. She looked up at her brother for support. "Right, Jerry?"

"Yeah," Jerry declared. Between the four of us, we can do this."

I remained unconvinced. "I don't know, you guys. Do you realize how big this is? Come on, a *Vodianoi* fixed on destroying the world! Maybe we should tell someone..."

The others appeared to consider this for a minute until Jerry piped up, "Okay. Well, how about this? If we find we can't do this on our own, we'll go to our parents. But first let's just see if we can do it solo."

Reluctantly, we finally agreed that we would at least try. Now we just had to retain the courage to put one foot in front of the other and put the plan into place.

If you recall, when we left Lessie (trapped inside her tree), all we knew was that Gwidon would provide us with the riddle *at some time.* We had no idea when. And so it was, with palpable anxiety on my part, we trudged toward the grove that held Lessie and her fallen tree, in hope combined with fear, that Gwidon and his riddle would be there.

The path, if you could call it that, looked like I imagine a Siberian highway must look. Rain sodden mud made a crushing blockade. Quitting the path, we steered our way purposefully between trees where we could, and managed at length to reach Lessie's arbutus tree prison. Rain fell ceaselessly, soaking us absolutely.

Being so close to where Lessie was hidden made me troubled to say the least. I gingerly touched the smooth, amber tree trunk exposed by the peeling bark and called out to her. A minute must have passed before I noticed that the others were searching the area around the tree. If Lessie answered my call, she went unheard.

Despite his calm exterior, Jerry announced, "Nope. It looks like no riddle arrived today."

My resolve was plummeting. "Oh, Jerry? Are you sure?"

"Yeah." He gave me a steady gaze, then added, "We'll try again tomorrow."

XV

IT WAS ON our third subsequent visit to Lessie's fallen tree that we saw it. Tacked haphazardly near the spot where Lessie's door once resided was a ragged sheet of parchment-like paper, stained, crumpled and sopping. What writing I could see from where I stood seemed unaffected by the bucketing rain.

What we'd been anticipating for these last few days was finally offered up to us. Unfortunately, it seemed that our wild thoughts and overworked imaginations had dampened everyone's drive. We eyed the document cautiously while taking furtive glances around us, each apparently fearful that our worst fears were to be realized with the unwelcome company of our tormentor. At length, secure in our private viewing, I gathered what bits of latent leadership I could, snatched the paper dramatically from the tree and began to read what was written to the group.

> "The closing of a door
> Causes nine to open.
> The closing of nine doors
> Causes one to open.
> What is it?"

And so, we were launched toward our first hurdle. By this time, the others had gathered warily behind me to read the words for themselves. Perhaps even Jerry considered our task insurmountable but he didn't let on. All he conceded was a "Well...I've got nothing – yet".

He wasn't the only one. No one apparently had any idea. After glancing back at the parchment I decided that the only thing I could do was simulate some of my customary assertiveness. "Okay guys. Here is what we do. We have one week, right? Well, let's brainstorm first and see where it gets us. It might lead to some important advance and then we go for it – Internet, books at home and library, follow hunches, anything we can come up with. We'll stay in close contact all week and get this done. You'll see."

Blank stares.

"Come on". I wasn't going to be defeated, especially now. "Lessie needs us. The world needs us". For some reason, at the word "Lessie" they all become more animated. Pity saving the world didn't elicit the same response but I guess some things are just too big for a bunch of kids.

"For Lessie." Rick placed his hand in the middle of our circle and the rest of us followed suit. Firmly meeting the backs of each other's hands, we shouted, "For Lessie!"

XVI

SO, I ASK you, dear reader, any ideas? No sweat. We didn't have any either – for a while.
"Door. What has a door?"

"No, Nine doors."

"Apartment. Office building."

"What else could be a door?"

"A door to the other side of something."

"Other side of what?"

You get the idea.

XVII

THE RAIN NEVER let up. The local news paraded footage of rising flood waters – devastation in some areas, analysis of poor environmental management as landslides were reported throughout the region and informed panels discussed the role global warming might be playing in all this. The riddle weighed mightily on my mind.

"So, have you guys come up with anything yet?" Rick asked. After freeing the riddle from Lessie's tree the day before, the four of us had hiked to Jerry's and Rita's house to make copies of it for all of us. After our free-for-all brainstorm, we decided to adjourn for the day as it was nearing supper-time. That night, Rick and I had wrestled with the riddle until my nerves were in tatters. I think we both felt overwhelmed and frankly scared. On the spot, we called Rita and made plans to meet with them at their house the next afternoon. This helped diffuse some of the pressure.

Rita was first to speak. "Well, I was thinking about what you said yesterday. You know 'a door to the other side' and all that and it got me thinking about life and death. The other side – heaven or whatever. What do you think? It was just a thought, but do you suppose I could be getting warm at least?"

Rick said, "Okay. Well, let's talk about this. Other side of life. Birth and death. Nine doors open when a door closes. What door? Nine open..."

"Hey, wait a minute. We may really be onto something." Jerry appeared energized. He stood and began pacing the room feverishly while the rest of us sat around their kitchen table watching him like chair umpires judging a tennis match. "Orifices. There are nine orifices on the human body. You know eyes, nostrils, ears, mouth, apertures for urine and feces." See, I told you he's quite the guy. Jack of Nine orifices and all.

"Okay," Rita said, taking back the baton from her brother. "So let's work with this. Nine orifices opening... when you are born – maybe. But what would be closing? Is it end of being unborn? The end of life in the womb? Hey, the closing of the umbilical cord...yes, I guess it could work. All right, that may explain the first part but what about the rest. Does it work?" Rita appeared guarded. She suddenly became intent on discovering the hidden mysteries of a discarded pen cap, careful to keep her eyes lowered. Rita will often think twice before saying anything so all of this so far had been an awesome demonstration.

I took the baton so my friend could recover. "The second part is nine doors close and one opens. I guess...death. The 'closing' of all 'orifices'..." I gestured the curved fingered air quotation sign for 'closing' and 'orifices'. I was perhaps a little out of my own comfort zone but had no intention of giving up now. "Death is a 'closing' of all these things and one opening must mean..." I took a moment to add my own brand of dramatic zeal. "The opening of Heaven's door." That had to be it. I felt quite proud of myself. I had worked through my earlier misery and felt that the riddle had been solved – of course with a little (a lot of) help from my friends. "I don't know about you guys but I think we've got it."

"I think you're right." I turned to scrutinize Rick who, until this moment, had remained silent. It wasn't so strange that he was quiet all this time. That happens a lot. He can be quite introverted when he wants to be. It was more that he actually admitted that I was correct about something. Normally, for him, this would be akin to eating Brussels sprouts. Not his favourite thing to swallow. But he smiled at me with almost...brotherly pride. It was quite the display. But, hey...I guess we were all pretty elated. The others wholeheartedly agreed with him.

"Well, does that mean we should head out to Lessie's tree? I...I don't know exactly how this works..."

I think we were all experiencing an adrenaline rush of some kind and felt driven to conquer our foe while we still felt this buoyancy. Without a word, we gathered our rain gear and steeled ourselves against the flood out-of-doors, armed with the parchment and our lately acquired grit. I hoped that was enough.

XVIII

A STEEL GREY world greeted us and rain poured down, soaking our bodies but fortunately, leaving our spirits intact. With determination, we marched the two blocks to the oceanside regional park. Our progress was delayed when we came to the plank stairs leading down to the beach. Looking out from our vantage point, it was apparent that the beach trail was inaccessible. A dark churning blanket of unrelenting surf obliterated our once peaceful sandy shore.

"We'll have to take the forest path," called Rick, shouting above the menacing growl of the waves. Wordlessly, we retraced our steps in order to gain entry to the woods at the far end.

The thickening forest cover provided some relief from the torrent, with rogue arbutus tree trunks offering the only colour visible amongst the grey mantle. With heads bowed to the elements and drooping branches, we painstakingly make our way to Lessie's fallen tree.

"Are you ready for this?" I asked Rick as I sidled up to him. He peered at me from beneath his drenched hood, his face the colour of paste. I gently touched his arm to offer some impression of reassurance. Regardless of everything, I still felt protective of my little brother.

At last, over a slight rise on the twisting, soggy trail we saw it. Lessie's home was exactly how we had left it last – abused and for all intents, abandoned. Half-heartedly we called to her fearing that our efforts were futile. Drumming rain provided a backdrop to these meagre attempts.

Nevertheless, our pleas had been heard. Rick's unsteady voice caused us all to freeze and turn his way. "Alex, what's that?" His voice had lost all strength and dripped panic.

I followed his stare and using all the self-control that I could muster stood fixed in place. Rising up from the moss-covered, saturated ground not 30 feet away was the form of a man... but I knew it could not possibly be called a man.

The *Vodianoi* approached us – he must have somehow sensed we had an answer to the riddle. I won't say he walked. His steps resembled the drifting performed by seagulls swimming on ocean waves. Noticeably, his feet never quite touched the ground.

He wore what looked like a seaweed-encrusted, okra-coloured cloak, tied with stinking reeds. It hung low enough to almost cover a pair of frayed, grey and grungy trousers. Scales coated his exposed arms. From his shoulder-length, raven-black hair hung dried fish heads and fish skeletons that looked to be tied on with bits of well-used fishermen's netting.

But it was to his face that my eyes unwillingly travelled. It appeared hard as sandstone but shone like the underside of a shell. It was his eyes that caused me to unwittingly quake. They looked human.

"I am Gwidon." That voice, like a whisper played backwards at speed, seemed to emanate from behind us. His thin, sallow lips failed to move.

"I...uh. I'm Alex," I managed to murmur, barely audible. "This is Rick, Jerry and Rita," I felt pinned in place.

"What do you have for me?" That voice again but this time it seemed to echo from the treetops above our heads.

"The riddle, I think we've solved the riddle." I was glad Jerry had marshalled some latent courage. My legs were beginning to break dance.

And then Gwidon restated the poem verbatim. I don't know if it was for dramatic effect or for some kind of weird, magic covenant. I only know that I was spellbound by the scene that played out in front of me.

"The closing of a door
Causes nine to open.
The closing of nine doors
Causes one to open.

What is it?"

With his final word, a tremendous thunderclap extinguished all other sounds. The quiet that followed was instantly filled with the amplified hammering of the tempest. A wind arose from the oceanside of the woods, levelling weaker saplings and bushes alike. I felt as if I was spinning uncontrollably within the vortex of the squall, clutching desperately to my wits with both hands, eyes tightly closed. Then, thankfully, I heard Jerry's voice above the din, out of breath and gasping.

"Is it a...a...lifetime?"

The wind ceased for a second, but then resumed instantly, only slightly diminished. I gingerly opened my eyes. The rain, though still falling, was slowing as if a valve from the heavens was being steadily closed. Gwidon stood tall before us as before but now an unseemly glow seemed to radiate from each of his scaly fingertips.

"It appears I have worthy opponents in this little...game." His eyes, unblinking, gleamed with apparent satisfaction. This time, the sound of his voice came from his direction but not necessarily from his mouth. His lips remained lifeless.

"What happens now?" Rita asked. She and Rick had stayed back until now. But now Rita moved closer to Gwidon with fresh determination.

"Well, your next riddle, of course," and from somewhere inside his cloak, Gwidon produced another weathered piece of parchment. "You have seven days." He handed it purposefully to Rita and then he began to waft backwards, backwards, until he reached the spot where he had at first emerged. At this point, still intent on us, he began to sink progressively deeper into the forest floor, steadily dissolving until he vanished altogether. And the rain fell – harder.

We gasped in shock and disbelief and then for some inexplicable reason, my mind turned to thoughts of Billy. Billy! Was I ever glad we had left him at home! I could just imagine the scene. The barking, the excitement, the tail wagging – Billy oblivious to any danger. Fluff and drool everywhere even in the abject rainstorm. I was intent on sharing my thoughts with the others in an attempt to ease some of the concentrated tension but all I managed was an unintelligible, "I've got to sit."

Following my lead, the others sank down to any remotely appropriate spot available, mindful of Lessie's tree, and gawked at each other in disbelief. I spied the fluttering of paper in Rita's hand. She was shaking.

I almost leapt when Jerry cleared his throat to speak. "Okay, let's see it." Rita handed the riddle to her brother without looking at him as Rick rose unsteadily and moved to read over Jerry's shoulder. Rita and I stayed planted where we were. I sat, willing myself to wake up from this decidedly unsettling dream.

After a minute or so, Rita asked her brother, "Well, what does it say?

XIX

MY MOM AND dad couldn't help but know that something was up. Disguising our anxiety and unease over the last few days was hopeless. The best Rick and I could do was attempt some impression of normalcy. The rain wasn't letting up and to complicate matters further, the winds were bordering on typhoon. We lost power more than once well, four times to be precise – as tree branches of all sizes were downed. Our stormglass barometer overflowed, creating a sickly, balsam stain on our kitchen linoleum.

My mom and dad are pretty good when it comes to respecting our need for privacy. Rick and I are lucky that way. But the day Rick got sick, well...you'll see.

We had somewhat recovered from the acute shock of the day we first met Gwidon, but in an impromptu teleconference, all of us agreed that a day's reprieve from riddle solving was in order – in the spirit of good mental health.

We had been out pretty much all afternoon, doing our best to see if we could locate Gwidon among the trees and bushes. Especially Billy. Even when we inspected the softened turf in the area surrounding Lessie's tree, there was no discernible trace of Gwidon ever having been there. There was no bruised ground, no disturbed moss – nothing. How he managed to disappear into nothingness like that left us bewildered.

Rick was particularly vexed. "There's got to be something." It appeared that he was absolutely fixed on being the one to discover something – anything. He bent down to check yet another fallen branch.

"Come on, Rick. Let's go home." I'd had enough. The search had somehow lost its zing with the unrelenting wind and the driving rain. "We have to get back or Mom will really start to wonder...and worry."

I knew Rick must have been tired, too. Since finally encountering Gwidon and having received the second riddle the day before, Rick had barely slept. He was pallid, ill-tempered and developing a cough.

With apparent effort, he climbed slowly to his feet and peered in my direction. He didn't look well at all.

"Let's get him home."

Rita and Jerry were more than ready, so gathering Rick in our clutches, we tramped our way out of the forest. After dropping off our friends at their home, Rick, Billy and I walked the remaining few blocks in silence. As we approached our drive, I steadied Rick to ease his way. I glanced up as our home came into view and noticed Mom's silhouette, backlit by the living room lamps, framed by the front window. It was barely 4:30 but it was already dark. Merciless rain will do that sometimes.

"Are you two okay?" Mom met us at the door and looked alarmed. "You guys were gone a long time. I even called Jerry's and Rita's mom to see if she had seen you."

"We're fine," I mumbled as I began the requisite towel tug-of-war dry-off fest with Billy. Man, does his coat hold water! Golden Retrievers!

"No, I don't think you are." She was peering at Rick. Grasping him firmly by the shoulders, she kissed his forehead to check his temperature. She tells us that's the best way to do it. "You're burning up." She briskly helped him remove his squelchy clothing and led him upstairs. "I want you to have a warm bath. I've got soup on the stove. It'll be ready by the time you come out."

"Thanks, Mom," he said and promptly started coughing.

I tried to make myself invisible while Rick had his bath but Mom managed to corner me in the upstairs hallway. Sternly, she began, "You know that I give you two a lot of privacy. And I trust you both to make good choices. I'm really disappointed by what I found here tonight. You were out all afternoon in this horrible weather and I'm sure Rick didn't *just* get sick this minute. Now tell me, what are you kids up to that would persuade you to push your limits like this?"

And there it was. The question from Mom that I'd been dreading for quite a while had now finally fallen into my lap with a terrible thud. I really didn't want to lie to her – she's, well...my mom -- but I also didn't want to get into the truth. It was all too fanciful, too fantastic to be believed. I knew I could never explain it properly. And, I admit, there was a large part of me that truly wanted to see if we could do this all on our own.

"Come on, out with it."

I blurted out, "We're working on a project." Where'd that come from?

"What project?"

I was thinking fast, "It's a group project with Jerry and Rita."

"What kind of project?"

This wasn't going well. Obviously, I didn't want to get into any specifics so I tried to divert the conversation with, "Don't worry, Mom. It's just a project. We'll both try to be more responsible in the future. I promise, Mom. I'm really sorry this happened."

This seemed to help quell my Mom's anxiety. "Okay," she said, "I trust you," and she gave me the type of hug only a mom can give. She pulled back, still holding my shoulders in her strong grasp and, looking at me intently, said, "But right now, Rick's health is my chief concern. He needs to rest. He's exhausted and sick. He needs to take it easy for a few days." She stood her ground, looking at me as if she was trying to see further into my head.

After what seemed an eternity, she smiled, apparently satisfied, and left to see about the soup. I let out the breath that I hadn't known I was holding. I knew she was worried and I confess, I felt like a complete heel. I turned to go after her, own up, come clean, but Rick – with a towel wrapped around his waist, having finished his bath early – headed me off before I could undo my web.

"I overheard you and Mom talking," he said in whispers, breathlessly. "Good job recovering from that project gaffe."

This did nothing to ease my conscience. "Just promise me, Rick. If this thing with Gwidon gets out of hand, we go to Mom and Dad."

"Promise."

At that, we moved to our separate corners. He made his way to his bedroom, still dripping from the bath, and I went to my room to change my clothes. Under my breath, to no one but myself, I said, "I hope this doesn't get too much crazier." I shrugged and went downstairs for soup.

XX

THE NEXT COUPLE of days, as expected, were spent indoors – out of the elements. Rick's cold turned out to be a minor bug and he seemed to pretty much mend with just a couple nights of uninterrupted sleep and a few days in dry environs. On the second day at home, Jerry and Rita came over, anxious to get to work on the riddle. Mom and Dad seemed satisfied that at least we were all inside, sheltered from the foul conditions escalating outside.

"Let's get cracking," Jerry said brusquely as he handed out copies of the riddle to each of us. "Time's running out."

That day, we chose to work in Rick's room. It's smaller than my bedroom but the light is better there. Rita and Rick claimed the side of his bed and Jerry and I sat on the floor at their feet.

"Okay, Jerry. Let's go. Read it out loud."

He read,

> "Science tries to quantify its
> Worth and hopes to borrow
> A trifle of its mighty force that
> Brings both joy and sorrow.
>
> Spirits rise to heights unknown or
> Souls are left to weep.
> It fills us with reflections of the
> Treasures that we reap.
>
> The mind at work in ecstasy
> The body can't deny.
> The snail and jellyfish don't know
> The joy of Passion's sigh.

What is it?"

"Yikes." I muttered. Upon hearing this riddle read aloud, the full realization of what we were facing hit me full in the face. "What the heck? How are we going to do this?" I cried out. "It sounds *a lot* harder than the previous riddle." Evidently, I wasn't in one of my unsinkable, self-assured mental states.

"Calm down, Alex." Jerry said. Did I sense a hint of irritation? "Rita and I have been working on this and I think we're already starting to get somewhere."

"Okay. Whatcha got?" Rick said, taking over while I sat, recovering my composure.

"Well, okay. Let's look at the second verse – I think it's the most straightforward. What causes spirits to rise to 'heights unknown' but also to weep? For me, it's all about music."

That's Rita of course. Music fanatic.

I had to admit it. It was at least a start. "So, is it about music in general or a specific kind of music or a specific song or what?"

Jerry said, "Well, after we got the music idea, then we looked more closely at the first verse. 'Science tries to quantify' – I thought that might refer to the Mozart Effect."

"Oh, yeah. I've read about that," Rick said. "Isn't that the theory that says you can increase a person's intelligence by playing Mozart's compositions? But really, come on! Is it possible?"

"Yeah, I know. I keep hearing conflicting reports. I'd like to believe it's true but even if it isn't, what remains is that music is still considered a potent force. They just don't know how to harness it. 'They' being well...scientists, I guess."

"This is great!" I thought we were really onto something. "So, do you think it's strictly music by Mozart?"

Rita piped up, "We're not sure. We were hoping to get your perspectives on this." She looked at Rick and me expectantly.

"Okay, let's see...well, I guess the third verse must hold the key," Rick said. "Alex, read it out loud again, will ya?"

So I did.

> "The mind at work in ecstasy
> The body can't deny.
> The snail and jellyfish don't know
> The joy of Passion's sigh."

We sat in reflection for a few moments but finally Jerry conceded, "No idea." He appeared utterly mystified.

I tried a shot at brainstorming. "What the heck do a jellyfish and snail have to do with music? It seems to be way out in left field. Is it a clue maybe? Rick, what do you think?"

"Let's see. Snail and jellyfish. Lower forms of life. Not capable of the emotion that is often tied with music. Physically simpler than us. What else?"

Rita said, "Is it possible we are taking it too literally? Is it possible that the snail and jellyfish are just symbols for something else?"

"Slow."

"Squishy parts."

"Invertebrates."

"I know, I know. We're back where we started. It was just a thought."

Rick threw out a lifeline, "I don't know, Rita. You may be on to something. The other day, I was leafing through a biology book Mom had borrowed from the library. Great pics, lots of little known facts and trivia on the natural world. I got quite a bit out of it. There was plenty of info on snails and jellyfish. Maybe we should look through it."

"Sounds good. Get the book."

We couldn't help but hear Rick rummaging through the pile of books lying at the foot of our bookshelf in the hallway outside his room. He re-emerged with a huge book, apparently part of a series of books, all devoted to invertebrates. "Man! Who knew there were so many?" I said, taking the book from Rick – who looked to be almost toppling with the weight of it – and leafing through page after page devoted to lower life forms.

I decided to turn to the beginning of the book in search of the Table of Contents. I ran my index finger down the page, stopping on a chapter entitled 'Jellyfish'. "Page 87," I said. Flipping to the right page, I began to read some of the more interesting headings they presented. "Compass Jellyfish, Lion's Mane Jellyfish, Medusa Jellyfish, Moon Jelly Jellyfish, Portuguese Man-Of-War..." I looked up, "What do you guys think? Is there any name that has a connection to Mozart or his work?"

Our resident classical music fiends looked at each other but shook their heads glumly.

Then Jerry suggested we look at the section on snails. Resolutely, I turned to the first page devoted to snails and began another recitation. "Amber Snail, Apple Snail, Banded Snail, Malayan Life-bearing Snail, Noonday Snail, Ramshorn Snail...Anything, you guys?" I asked hopefully.

Rita moaned, "I'm sorry. This is getting us nowhere."

I was just as frustrated. There were just too many possibilities. It was overwhelming. And it seemed that nothing could be tied to Mozart in any way.

"I wonder if it's just a red herring," Rick said. "You know, designed to throw us off the scent. Maybe the answer is just...music."

Silence followed as we all considered this.

Finally, Jerry shook his head, "No. No, I don't buy it. If it was that simple, it would be one verse not three. There's definitely more to it than that."

"But what?"

I think we were all feeling pretty beleaguered and frankly, I was weary. I felt like we were doing little more than wasting our time, chasing dead ends. With the magnitude of what we were trying to accomplish hanging over our heads, I was beginning to feel hopeless. And to make matters worse, each day seemed to present worsening weather conditions -- intermittent fog, rain and wind. The fact that they seemed so out of control only served to fuel my anxiety.

But on a purely personal level, what weighed most heavily on my mind was Lessie's welfare. I wondered how she was coping, what she was feeling, how she would survive being trapped inside that tree for so long. Even though I understood she isn't made quite like us. I felt very close to her and I was worried. So yes, I was thankful when Rita suggested we take a break for the rest of the day.

XXI

DURING THIS LAST while of so much upheaval, I began to notice a subtle change in Rick. Don't get me wrong, he was still totally capable and willing to drive me batty, but at times, there appeared to be a new seriousness about him that frankly, I didn't recognize.

Here's an example of what I mean. After Jerry and Rita went home that day, I was anxious to regain some of the light-heartedness of my former life but Rick only wanted to work on the riddle some more. I managed to distract him for a while with a board game we'd both enjoyed in the past, but Rick's heart was clearly not in it. Within ten minutes, Rick retired to his room armed with every science book we owned. And it wasn't until nearly nine o'clock that night that I noticed his light turn out.

I, on the other hand, forced into solitude, spent the rest of the day trying to escape – reading a novel that I had not picked up since, coincidently, before Lessie had been imprisoned. Well, at least it looked like I was reading – nothing was sticking.

XXII

THE NEXT AFTERNOON, Rick and I walked those two eternally familiar blocks to Rita's and Jerry's house. Armed with nothing but the shaky optimism gained from our half-day break from overt tension, we rang their doorbell and were (thankfully) ushered out of the veritable monsoon outside.

We exchanged greetings but quickly moved to their kitchen table to get to work. Time was relentlessly ticking away.

"Anything?" I asked.

"Oh, Alex," Rita sighed, "sadly, no." She was visibly distressed. Yet although she was pale as a blanched almond, her chin was set with purpose.

"We don't have any leads either. What now?"

Rick took a moment to read through his copy of the riddle again and then replied, "You know, I spent all night yesterday researching every conceivable invertebrate I could find and you know what? I think I was chasing up the wrong squidgy thing. Look, here on the last line. 'Passion' is capitalized. Why would that be?" He looked at each of us in turn. I thought he might be onto something but I had no idea what.

"Wait a minute. Let me see that." Rita grabbed the paper from his hands and read aloud, "'the joy of Passion's sigh'. I know what that is. At least I think I can narrow down our search considerably." She was a transformed girl – animated, flushed, beaming. "It's not Mozart. We were wrong. It's Bach, J. S. Bach. It's one of *his* pieces. Either St. John Passion or St. Matthew Passion."

"Get out of here!" I exclaimed. "Really?"

"Yeah, it fits! Music. Joy. Passion. I can feel it. People, we are on our way!"

Now it was Jerry's turn to crank it up. "But how do we determine which piece works with the riddle?"

And it was Rick who led us on. "Jerry, fire up the Internet."

In minutes we had our answer. Recalling what he had learned from his research the day before, Rick tried various search combinations and then – drum roll...Medusa Jellyfish, snail and St. Matthew Passion!

"What? Are you kidding me? It's there?" I couldn't believe it. It was all too much. I almost wept.

"Yes! It's from a collection of essays by Dr. Lewis Thomas. In one of them, he talks about Bach's St. Matthew Passion in terms of being akin to listening to the brain. Music, he says, is how we explain how the human mind works. The book's called...are you ready for this? *The Medusa and the Snail: More Notes of a Biology Watcher.* Riddle solved!"

XXIII

MUD SPLATTERED OUR boots as we threaded our way through the arbutus grove, single file, to Lessie's fallen tree. We had raced from Jerry's and Rita's home feeling upbeat, almost cocky, giddy and relieved beyond words. But as we neared our destination, the importance of the true state of affairs began to eat at our fragile confidence.

Through the curtain of heavy rain, we saw that Lessie's tree lay as before and the surrounding area was as we had left it – but with one disquieting inconsistency. A grizzled shape with its back to us leaned heavily against an arbutus stump. Not audacious enough to take another step, we halted, aware of its identity.

Gwidon, of course.

Our approach, however, had not gone unnoticed. The form rose laboriously from its stupor, as if in physical pain. He turned slowly to face us. He was barely suspended above the muddy forest floor. His expression was still. His eyes, lethargic.

Rick was the first to regain his ability to speak. "Gwidon, we have an answer."

With effort, Gwidon challenged, "That may be, but is it the right answer?" He shifted his weight from side to side. Outwardly, he appeared to have nothing physically wrong. But something was definitely up. A groan came from deep within him but he continued by reciting the second poem without moving his lips. "What is it?" he concluded. His voice rose to the forest canopy.

And so, the moment had arrived – again. Were we right to limit our answer to St. Matthew Passion and not music in general? Well, we had to aim high – so much depended on it.

Enter Rita. "St. Matthew Passion," she said with clear, precise enunciation.

She didn't even flinch when Gwidon, without bothering to meet her eyes, replied in a voice that seemed completely void of emotion, "Well, well. Interesting. Not just music." He paused to lift his head, searching our faces for what, I will never know. And then, to our palpable relief, he ended with, "I thought I had you with this one." His voice seemed to come from behind us and trailed off with formless resonance.

We smiled our relief. A crackling thunder swelled as rain pelted down. Gwidon reached inside his clothing. "Your next riddle."

Stunned, I timidly moved forward to take it from him. Unwillingly, my eyes drifted to his and became locked there in his concrete stare. His eyes, though hard, betrayed something I never imagined I'd see. Yes, I was sure of it. His eyes showed emotion – hopelessness, torment, or maybe something more? What was it? Desperation?

"Gwidon?" I said, my voice barely audible, even to myself.

And then his masked bearing crumbled slightly and he smiled – weakly – but still, I considered it a smile, even though his lips didn't move. The smile was in his eyes. The raging storm momentarily softened its thunderous roar. His face, although it never lost its translucent pearling, changed its quality from stone to glass – and became vulnerable. Without speaking again, he dropped his gaze, withdrew, backing up slowly while he floated until he disappeared, back down into the forest floor once more.

The next sound I was aware of was Rita calling me home. I felt her put her arm around my shoulders as she turned me to walk with her. Mechanically I placed the riddle in my raincoat pocket, unread.

XXIV

BILLY'S ENTHUSIASTIC GREETING nearly knocked the wind from me but at least it functioned to turn me toward the vicinity of my normal self – albeit abruptly. He frantically sniffed at my outer clothing and proceeded to jump up and prod my pocket with his wet snout.

"Hmm, it looks like Billy missed you two." Mom was leaning against the wall in the mudroom entrance, arms crossed, grinning.

I did my best to appear nonchalant as I pushed Billy's nose away from my pocket and went to hang up my jacket.

Rick expertly drew Mom's attention from my face and, taking her about the waist, moved her toward the kitchen. "What's for supper? I'm starved!"

I could just barely hear her reply, "Well, I'm glad to hear you have an appetite." I had taken the stairs two at a time to gain some distance from perceptive eyes and thankfully received the solace I so desperately needed within the inner sanctity of my bedroom. Minutes passed. I sat on my bed, still a little dazed but recovering.

Eventually, I made my way to the bathroom and looked at my face in the medicine cabinet mirror. Yeah, I thought so. I looked...well...changed. My whole impression of Gwidon had been altered and what I thought I'd known had become obsolete. This strange creature, this *Vodianoi* of all things, might actually be something to be well...protected – not feared. I knew this line of thinking should have been inconceivable, but there it was. I breathed deeply to gain some self-control and splashed water on my face. It didn't help much. Well, what could I do? I took one last look in the mirror and marched downstairs to try my hand at appearing as normal as possible one more time.

XXV

THE FOLLOWING AFTERNOON, Rita and Jerry met up with Rick and me at the local library. It's not a very big place but its impact is mighty. Ivy creeps up its outer walls slowly acting to camouflage the unassuming red brick one-storey building. When you make your way inside, the two automatic opening doors part like curtains to grandly present row on row of book shelves chock full to bursting. The section devoted to children's literature alone is humbling. Rick and I had been coming here nearly five years, ever since we moved to our present house. The building itself may not be much, but it feels like an extension of our home and I must say, the staff really go out of their way to help.

We had just settled ourselves down at a free table that we'd found near the back of the main reading room and I was just pulling out the latest riddle when we heard someone call out, "Hey! Hi you guys!"

We looked up all at once to see our friends, Sasha and Lex peeking at us from behind a display case. They're sisters who we've known for a few years now. They moved here from Holland (I think, it's Holland. They have some kind of lilting accent) and they're also homeschooled. We probably see them about once every month or so at various homeschooling functions.

Sasha's 13 and older than her sister by about six years and pretty much runs the show. She's really very pretty in an exotic kind of way. She has olive skin – flawless – and her eyes are a cobalt blue. Her hair is totally unruly like an Italian opera singers and is usually tied back "to keep small birds out of it," as she says. Her sister is still finding her look, of course – she's just seven – but she has an uncommon beauty as well.

"So good to see you!" I stood up quickly and hugged both girls. It had been a while.

"Nice weather, huh?"

All of us laughed uneasily. The remorseless tempest was both threatening and depressing. It stood as a constant reminder of our dire mission.

"We haven't seen much of you lately," Sasha continued. "What have you four been up to?"

Without pausing to think, I said, "We've been busy with life, I guess – you know, homeschool stuff, swimming lessons, various uh...projects." I bit my lip but not before a shot in the ribs from Rick who sat to my right. I was still holding the riddle.

"Projects? Are you working on one today? What kind of project is it?"

Why I said anything about projects (again!) I'll never know. I guess I have to work harder on that 'thinking before you speak' stuff.

Thank goodness for Rita. "What about you two? How's your riding going?" She shot me a reassuring glance as she said this and then smiled innocently back at Sasha. Both girls were horse-mad and I think Rita knew that this would be a good diversion.

"Oh, it's great!" Sasha gushed. "Lex even has her first competition in three weeks. Jenny says she's more than ready. And I've been getting into western riding lately. I just love barrel-racing. Oh, and the tack. It reminds me of the leather craft that I...anyway, I'm getting side-tracked, what project are you working on? I'm curious." She glanced furtively at the parchment I had been holding that was now lying face down on the table.

"Is your mom here?" I asked. "Our moms went to the gym next door." My attempt at a rerouting of attention.

"No, I'm right here." It was their mom, Sophia. She appeared behind the girls and greeted us all individually, cheerful as always. She's super nice.

"Hi, Mom."

"I'm sorry, girls, but we have to get going. We've got that rally to get to." They're a pretty environmentally-minded family and often participate in public assemblies.

Without hesitation the girls sang out, "Bye!" and turned to leave. I thought I was in the clear and had already diverted my eyes from the others when I heard Sasha call across the room,

"Alex, I guess I'll have to phone you later about that mysterious project."

I waved sheepishly as Sasha, Lex and Sophia exited through the closing automatic doors.

The others stared at me with arms crossed. "What?" I said. "It went okay...sort of." All right. You called it. I was being a bit defensive.

"Alex, the fewer people that know about our 'project' as you call it, the better." Jerry was plainly irked.

Rita patted my arm. "Don't worry, Alex, it will probably all blow ever. What's done is done. Don't dwell on it."

"But what am I going to tell her when she calls? I mean, it's Sasha! She's such a good friend." I stopped to think, "Maybe..."

Rick stopped me, "Alex, don't even consider it."

"She wouldn't..." I began, but Rick cut me off.

"No, Alex. We don't know what the exact rules of this whole thing are. Lessie's life may be put in further danger if we involve others. To say nothing of the planet. This is just too important to take any chances."

"What are you two talking about?" asked Rita.

"Alex wants us to let Sasha in on the secret."

I interjected, "She wouldn't tell anyone else. Well, except Lex, I guess. But that's it. She might even be of some help. These riddles are pretty difficult and are only getting harder."

"I think the best thing to do would be to avoid letting more people in on this. Like Rick said, we don't know the rules for sure. Gwidon seems pretty unstable and we don't know how he would react if we changed things up."

"Okay. Fair enough, Rita. I won't say anything about our secret. I don't know what I'm going to tell Sasha when she calls though. Or *if* she calls. Maybe she won't call at all." I was grasping for any flotation device I could find. "Let's just solve these riddles and save the world." I said this rather dramatically. Wouldn't you? "Then I won't be faced with this dilemma."

Jerry said, "Now you're talking. Alex, read the next riddle."

I wasn't sure if my inner resolve was equal to my external bravado but I obediently grabbed the parchment, straightened its edges and read,

> "The colour made when berry-lobbed
> Is worth a second checking.
> I will give you one more clue:
> A word is intersecting.
>
> You will use this letterbox
> To aid in further fishing.
> You all know the primaries,
> Find the one that's missing.

And I guess this is the letterbox," and I handed the parchment to Jerry. It looked like this:

> DOREB
> OBRYE
> RRLRB
> EYRBB
> BEBBD

"Okay," he said, "let's get started."

XXVI

"ALEX, COME AND eat." My mom's voice broke my daydream. Ever since my last encounter with Gwidon I couldn't concentrate. At the library that afternoon, although I don't think anyone noticed my preoccupation, my mind kept wandering to him and how he had looked at me. Could it really be true? Could he really be in some way vulnerable and not quite as evil as we all presumed?

As a result, I hadn't been much help to my fellow riddle-solvers. But the others had been able to unearth a couple of things:

1.   Our real challenge was at the end of the poem. Contained somewhere within the workings of the riddle were two of the three primary colours. We all knew the primary colours (yellow, red and blue) and our task was to find which one was missing.

2.   We were also given that pretty cryptic letterbox. Nevertheless, we did think it was neat how the "words" intersected each other in order horizontally and vertically.

We spent the rest of our time poring over the letterbox trying to figure out the "word is intersecting" part (see line four) and any connection we could find with the three primary colours.

We didn't make much headway so we made copies of the poem and the letterbox and opted to work on them independently at our respective homes.

Only now, Mom was calling me down for supper and I had hardly unpacked my books from the library let alone made any progress on the riddle. Rick had been working quietly in his room ever since we got home. I wondered how he was making out, but I was pretty sure I would find out soon.

XXVII

THE NEWS WAS bordering on calamitous. Extensive flooding, people left homeless, power outages everywhere. The Coast Guard had been called out to help rescue people. Meteorologists were positively giddy. They had never been given so much air play. And they were having a heck of a time predicting when this "low-pressure weather pattern" would break up. Forecasting the weather is a dicey enterprise at the best of times but, with what was happening in the skies over our area these days, prediction was virtually pointless. Each day, it just got worse with little or no warning. Everyone was talking about it — except the four of us. We remained mute, willing the outside world to recede while we worked on what we needed to work on, but it was getting increasingly difficult. However, we reasoned that, even if we did tell all that we knew, first of all, would anyone believe such a fantastic tale? And second, what could be done to stop the force causing it?

We were solving the riddles quite handily on our own — and on time. Adding other people to the mix might jeopardize the agreement with Gwidon and create a bigger problem than what we were dealing with now. And it seemed unlikely to us that others could do much better. Secretly, I got the impression that it was becoming a matter of pride for us. After all, we were just kids and look how well we were doing. Two down, two riddles to go and our world would be saved and Lessie would be freed — at least we hoped she would be freed.

Rick and I walked doggedly, heads bowed to the driving wind and rain, determined to make good time to Jerry and Rita's house. The urgency was plain. Time seemed to be steadily draining away and through all that had happened to us so far, one fact was clearly emerging: we were much more effective when we worked together.

Rick and I arrived at their door and were swiftly ushered into their warm home. We shed our outer clothes, making puddles on the floor, and warmed our hands by their woodstove. Their mom had gone grocery shopping and their dad was at work, so we took over their kitchen table, eager to get to the job at hand.

Rita started us off with, "I couldn't find any word in that jumble of letters. There just weren't enough useful vowels or something. But I did look more closely at the poem. I think we may have been wasting our time. Here, look."

She pulled out her copy of the riddle and pointed to the first line. "'The colour made when berry-lobbed'. Isn't that an odd word – 'berry-lobbed'? Why is that line even there in the first place? It's kind of suspicious. We know the primary colours."

"Well, let's see." Rick piped up. "Berries come in all kinds of colours but we are only interested in blue, yellow and red. And lobbed means thrown, right?"

"Right," the rest of us chorused.

Rick continued, "The colours made when different types of berries are thrown."

"Yes, but wait a minute," Rita said. "'A word is intersecting'...maybe one of the words in the *poem* is the one that is intersecting. Maybe 'Berry-lobbed'".

What?

"You know, the hyphen could signify an intersection."

"Rita, that's great." I think we were all pretty impressed but was it the breakthrough we had been looking for?

And then Jerry added his sober input, "The letterbox. We need to figure out how the letterbox fits into this before we get too carried away."

I was taken aback. It was my brother who, without hesitation, provided the answer. "Simple. The letters likely match up with the letters in 'berry-lobbed'. If you write the word horizontally and vertically and position them so that they intersect at the L..." He moved Rita's paper closer, wrote out an intersecting berry-lobbed and matched each letter in the letterbox with the corresponding letter in the intersecting words – twice, leaving four extra letters -- R, B, B, and R.

Rick stopped. Put the pen down. Looked up. Grinned his grin. "Yellow."

"What? Really?" I was bowled over and full of pride at the same time.

"Yellow. R, B, B and R. Two R's and two B's. Two reds and two blues. What's missing? Yellow!"

"Are our jackets dry yet?" I asked. Not that it mattered.

XXVIII

JERRY AND RITA'S mom came home just as we were leaving. We stopped long enough to help her get the groceries into the house, mumble something about needing some fresh air, and hurtle ourselves out into the pouring rain.

The forest path had become almost impassable. In places, we sank in squelchy mud to the tops of our gumboots. Not surprisingly, we met no one else braving the wooded path or, for that matter, the elements. With perseverance, we made it to Lessie's tree in good time. My face would have glowed with perspiration if it were not for the rain streaming down onto it.

Gwidon must have sensed our approach for, within moments of our arrival, we witnessed his creepy ascent from the recesses of the earth.

"Quite timely, I see." His voice came from near my left shoulder but he stood (or rather, hovered) right in front of me. He looked as he had when I had last seen him – weary and burdened. Could he be sick?

Rick moved to stand between Gwidon and me – I guess he can be protective of me too.

Gwidon's head dropped slightly, almost as if he were weakened and then without warning, he began to recite the verses from the last riddle. He finished with, "What is the answer to this riddle?"

Rick stood, looking proud, tall and confident. "Yellow."

"Well...done." Gwidon faltered and would have fallen to the forest floor if Lessie's tree had not been right behind him when he stumbled.

Without thinking, I rushed to help him. I came within inches of him but something stopped me from actually touching him. All I could manage was, "Gwidon! Are you...all right?" I became aware of the others staring at my back in a state of disbelief.

They seemed to be asking me what the heck I was doing. I realized then that I scarcely knew myself.

He sat heavily on Lessie's fallen tree, hunched over as if to catch his breath – even though he didn't appear to breathe. As he sat immobile, the heavy rain began to lighten and a dull glow tried to break through its dreary burden. But as soon as I became aware of this transformation, the leaden curtain returned and the torrent began once more, though now even more fiercely. This occurred quickly, yes, but not before I confirmed my suspicion. Gwidon's eyes. At one point, when he was prone against Lessie's fallen tree, he looked right through me and I know I saw it. His humanity. I was sure of it.

And then, fiercely, from the depths of his cloak, he wrenched out what I believed to be the final riddle. He shoved it at me roughly and rose, steadied himself impatiently and announced, "You have seven days." He turned and soared – though unsteadily – to his peat-covered refuge and disappeared with a flash of lightning.

XXIX

I WAS STAGGERED. I knew Rick, Jerry and Rita were speaking softly to each other ahead of me on the trail but no one said a word to me during that long walk home. At their door, Rita invited us to her house the next day but seemed to not be able to make eye contact with me. We left them in their doorway and moments before our house came into sight, Rick grabbed my arm and cried out, "Alex, what got into you?"

"I...I don't know. I..." My mind was racing. "Do you think I made matters worse?" I stopped and looked up at the sky and as I did, a bolt of lightning flashed.

"Well, you didn't help any!" Rick was clearly distressed. "Let's just hope we can solve this riddle and fast."

When we got home, Dad met us at the door. "Alex, Sasha just called. She wants you to call her back."

XXX

THE WIND SEEMED to be threatening to lift our house from its foundation. An eerie moan reverberated through neighbouring trees evoking images of uncontrolled rage. Billy hadn't left my mom's side all evening, whimpering softly, and cowering now and then. Mom and dad thought it best that we all sleep downstairs this night. The wind was liable to uproot nearby trees standing in sodden ground. Weather reports provided evidence that we were in the grips of the "storm of the century". Funny. I recall that, just a few years ago, a similar tempest had risen up and they called *that* the "storm of the century" too. I was considering this as Rick and I got our makeshift beds in order on the floor in front of the fireplace. Then we lost power. If only the howling coming from our woods were as stilled as our electrical appliances.

We were unable to sleep. Mom and I huddled together by an old-fashioned oil lamp that we had bought at an auction house late last summer. The poor lighting and our threadbare nerves made reading unproductive. Sickening crashes emitted now and then from our back woods. Rick and I would periodically look toward the rear of our property but the faint outline of the forest offered little key to which trees had been ripped out. Toward three o'clock, sleep finally provided release from the tragedy unfolding beyond our doors.

XXXI

A LIGHTENING OF the sky indicated that the sun had ascended though the actual orb remained unseen through the murkiness of a bucketing day. I woke abruptly and looked out to our back-yard. I stared in disbelief at the destruction of our woods. One-hundred-year-old trees – uprooted and tossed like discarded refuse. Great mounds jutted 25 feet into the air where roots lay exposed. Trees lay like fallen dominoes. Vacant tracks were created as evidence of the wind's command.

Mom and dad were relieved that, aside from a few long branches that had hit the house, we had made it through the storm largely unscathed. Even our old, reliable half-ton waited patiently outside with no real damage. It seemed that the woods had taken the brunt of the storm's fury on our behalf. I let Billy out for his morning fête but he wasn't his typical raring-to-go self. He came back in after only a minute, evidently thankful to return to the security of home. The power remained out so I poured myself a bowl of cold cereal and joined my family at the kitchen table.

Dad announced, "After I finish eating, I'll head out to see if the neighbours need any help. They may not have fared as well as we did."

"I'll come with you," Mom said. But then she looked from Rick to me and stated, "I want you two to stay indoors for now. There's still a risk of falling branches. It's still pretty blustery out there."

I wanted to stay in anyway, but tried to make my voice sound reluctant when I muttered, "Okay." Rick and I needed to talk. It hadn't just been the storm that had kept me from falling asleep that night.

The door had just closed behind mom and dad when Rick, with aching calm, said "Gwidon did this."

I admit it, the thought had occurred to me too. But instead of confessing that to Rick, I said, "We don't know that for certain. Yeah, it seems that since Gwidon trapped Lessie the weather has steadily gotten worse every week but this was so...drastic."

Something in me refused to believe that this was solely Gwidon's work. "Come on, Rick. Isn't it possible that this was just another one of these rogue storms that have been happening more and more lately – that have nothing to do with Gwidon? Remember what we learned in that lecture at the university?" I looked at Rick beseechingly.

I expected him to either agree with me that at least I had a point or counter my argument with more evidence of Gwidon's foul nature. Instead, Rick surprised me by saying, "You know, Alex. You seem different." He shook his head and levelled his eyes on me. "Ever since we saw Gwidon that last time...before all this." He glanced out the window at the destruction.

"Oh yeah, in what way?" I breathed carefully, casting my eyes downward.

"You're...I don't know, kind of protective of Gwidon, I guess. You *did* ask him if he's all right. What do you care, anyway? It would be better for us if he wasn't."

I tried to gain some courage. "I just think it's not quite so cut and dried. Gwidon seems so...vulnerable – not quite the evil being we'd thought he was." I shrugged my shoulders and looked at him hopefully.

He wasn't so easily persuaded. "That's crazy. Look what he's done," he said, gesturing all around in disgust.

"I just don't believe all this was Gwidon's doing!" I was getting frustrated and defensive. "Why don't we discuss this later with Rita and Jerry?" I wasn't sure I wanted this either but it felt like a good ploy to stall for time.

Although Rick looked reluctant, he said, "Deal."

XXXII

I FELT REALLY bad about not calling Sasha back before the storm took our power. This was compounded when the power remained off for days but I reasoned that, when you considered all the damage meted out on the area, Sasha was most likely okay with my not calling. Her family might be dealing with bigger problems.

Mom and dad had insisted that we stay in the house until things settled down outside. But, it wasn't just the threat of falling branches that kept us indoors. With more than a few roads closed because of toppled trees, and power lines down all over the area, a state of emergency had been declared.

We felt isolated from everyone – especially Rita and Jerry – but I guess that couldn't be helped. We were so accustomed to seeing our friends every day or so, it was a bit of a shock to be without our regular refuel. But more importantly, we had a riddle to solve and not much time remaining, so Rick and I had no choice but to work on it without them.

"Okay, Alex, read it out loud."

"I am both the sun and moon
When dark becomes the light.
All and none are part of me.

73

I'm blind and yet have sight.

Man and woman, young and old,
I'm here and also there.
I can't be found in every space
Yet I am everywhere.

I can die yet truly know
My immortality.
I am tied to future, past,
Where present longs to be.

Devil's pawn and angel's seed,
The yin and yang of me
Reminds me that I change with time
Yet your eyes won't see.

What am I?"

I searched Rick's face for a lifeboat but found the boat was sinking fast.

XXXIII

IT TOOK A leap of faith but by the next day we had recovered *some* clarity. We really just had to consider that ultimately, it might be solely up to Rick and me to solve this riddle. There was no telling how long we would be holed up at home, without power, without telephone. Even cell phones were out of the equation – no power to recharge their batteries. Taking a commiserate deep breath, Rick and I put our collective shoulders to the challenge and steeled ourselves for whatsoever might come to pass – the alternative was unimaginable.

By the third day without power, it had come to this:

"What do you think 'I'm blind and yet have sight' means?" By now, I had gone over the riddle so many times that I thought *I* was going blind.

"I thought maybe insight, you know, I'm blind but I still understand."

"But what about being both the sun and the moon? They are totally different things. One is a gigantic fireball and the other is a frozen rock."

"I know. And how can something be young and old...or man and woman, come to think of it?"

We were getting nowhere. In frustration, I tossed my pen on Rick's desk, sat back and rubbed my eyes. I needed a timeout. Leaving Rick to persist in this torment, I stood and made my way downstairs to check the pantry for a snack and as I reached the door...Hooray! The power came back on in mechanized ecstasy.

"Yahoo!" I cried out. Ah, that familiar hum of the refrigerator!

Mom, who'd been in the living room reading quietly, threw down her book, grinned and ran to give me a warm hug, "Oh, happy day!" she exclaimed. "Now we can all get back to normal."

"Yeah, it's good isn't it?" I guess we were all very relieved.

"I bet you are itching to call Sasha back." She walked to the phone, presumably to confirm a dial tone.

"Oh yeah. Yeah. I will...a little later." I backed out of the area like I had seen a mountain lion and trudged back upstairs to

Rick's room, head down. Okay. I admit it. I was lily-livered. But really, Sasha was my good friend and I hated the thought of deceiving her. It was bad enough I had left mom and dad out of the loop. I entered the sanctity of Rick's room and shut the door behind me. He had taken my place at his desk and was evidently still engaged in riddle-wrestling.

I opened with, "Power's back on."

"Yeah, I know," Rick said, distracted. "Look at this." He moved the parchment so I could see it and pointed at the last line, 'I change with time yet your eyes won't see'. "It's the only line that is different. You know...no real opposites. What changes with time that we don't notice?"

"I don't know." I was still rattled and couldn't concentrate on the riddle right at that minute. "Mom just stopped me downstairs and reminded me to call Sasha. I feel so bad, Rick. I should call her, but..."

"What are you going to say when she asks about the project?"

"That's just it. I don't know."

At that moment, I heard the phone ring downstairs and my heart nearly stopped. I listened intently. Finally, I heard my Mom's voice call, "Alex. It's Rita."

I looked at Rick and sighed in utter relief. A stay of execution. My call to Sasha could be delayed...for now anyway.

XXXIV

HI GUYS!" RITA called out. She opened their front door just as we'd stepped on to their pebbly driveway. Once we were safely inside, we all began to talk at once like ducks at feeding time. Rick and I took off our gear and were ushered straight away to Rita's room. Four chairs had been carefully set up around a small wooden table. It looked like Jerry and Rita were ready for some serious riddle-cracking. I hoped I was up to it.

Earlier, when I had rushed downstairs to take her call, I knew I had to make plans to see her and Jerry. The days of house arrest were chafing me something awful. And I was pretty sure Mom would say it was okay. When I got to the phone and heard Rita squeal "Hello," I was both delighted and relieved. I wasn't sure how she was feeling about me since our last encounter with Gwidon. But yes, she wanted us to come over so everything was okay. Holding the phone in both hands, I begged Mom to let us go. Happily, her response was a "Yes!" but with the caveat, "Bundle up. It's still pretty miserable out there."

I hung up the phone and bellowed for Rick to come down. We gathered our things like a trumpet blast went off and braced for the hammering black rain. The riddle was tucked away safely in my hip pocket.

Now, settled at their table, I dug the crumpled riddle from my pocket and handed it to Jerry. He made copies for everyone and took a moment to read it out loud to the group. Rick and I offered what little we had deduced.

"All these things are opposites. Yin and yang, devil and angel, dying and immortality. Hmmm..."

"Wait, you know, maybe that's it...opposites. But that doesn't explain the last line. You know," I pointed, "changing with time. Opposites are always opposites, aren't they?" I was thinking fast.

The others joined in on my guesswork but pretty soon it became obvious that we had reached a stalemate. We decided to take a short break. At this point, Rita drew me away from the others.

"Alex, I want to talk to you...about Gwidon."

"Yeah?" Unfortunately I had a good idea where this was heading. I'd thought I could avoid it but clearly, I couldn't.

"I mean, I think you stepped over a line or something because...well...look outside. Look what Gwidon did."

"Not you, too? Like I was telling Rick, I'm not convinced Gwidon did all of this. Over the last few years we've been having a lot of bad storms. Yes, this is worse than before, but I just can't believe Gwidon would do this."

"What? Are you crazy?" Her voice was rising. "A bit worse? You can't believe Gwidon would do this? Of course he would do this! It's cataclysmic out there and has been for weeks – because of him! He's trapped Lessie! What more proof do you want?"

"Rita, stop! You didn't see what I saw. I saw his eyes. They were...vulnerable."

"Alex, I can't believe you!"

She stopped. I think she was unwilling to take this to the next level but I had heard enough. Presenting a calmness I didn't feel, I said, "Rita, I just don't see him that way. I think I'd better go."

She made no move to stop me. I walked out of the room, ignoring the boys' gaping mouths. With the riddle a crumpled mess in my fist, I grabbed my jacket and marched into the dim light of a miserable day's late afternoon, and I cried all the way home.

XXXV

RITA AND I had never had a fight like this before. Never! How could two people who got along so well, see things so differently? She was one of my best friends and I feared that I had lost her forever.

When Rick straggled home, he was withdrawn. He knew what the argument was about and I think he was pretty taken aback by the outcome. I told him I didn't want to talk about it and thankfully, he let it go at that. He went up to his room and closed the door behind him leaving me to my turbulent thoughts.

At the supper table that night, I strove to act like my old self but clearly it didn't work. After Rick had washed the dishes and I was just putting away the last of the clean glasses, Mom cornered me. "Alex, I know something is wrong. What is it, honey?"

Reluctantly, I relented, "Rita and I had a fight."

"Oh, Alex! I'm so sorry. Can I ask what happened?"

"You know, Mom, I don't want to talk about it...not yet. Give me a little time."

"Fair enough. You know you can talk to me about anything, right?"

"I know, Mom. Thanks. I love you," and I hugged her tight in a sad attempt to take away some of the pain in my heart.

XXXVI

TIME WAS SLIPPING away. It was the night before we were to meet Gwidon by Lessie's tree and give him the answer to the final riddle. I hadn't even looked at the riddle since Rita and I'd had our falling-out, and Rick was keeping his distance from me too. He'd been going to Jerry's and Rita's house every afternoon, but seemed to return each day, looking disheartened.

I was in my bedroom, on my bed, book in hand. My eyes moved over the words on the page, one by one as if I was reading...but I couldn't put the words together. Concentration was absolutely beyond me. It wasn't until the phone rang that I realized I had been listening for it. My heart rejoiced at the sound as I raced downstairs, hopeful that it was Rita.

I managed to get the phone on the third ring. "Hello?" Practically gasping.

It was Sasha.

"Oh, Hi. I've been...meaning to call you. How are you?" I said, trying to disguise my disappointment.

"Alex, are you okay? You don't sound great." Apparently, I hadn't done a very good job at masking how I felt.

"Oh...well...Rita and I had a fight." I came clean.

"What? Over what? You guys are inseparable."

I felt weak. "I know."

She hesitated and then said, "Alex...is it something to do with that project you're working on?"

Emotionally, I was on the verge of collapse and my resolve was severely weakened. "Sasha, I don't want to talk about this over the phone. It's too...big. Can you come by sometime and I'll tell you...everything."

"Sure. Let me ask my mom. I'll call you tomorrow."

XXXVII

I DIDN'T SLEEP much that night. The realization that we may very well fail, that Lessie would be lost to us forever, that Gwidon could end up destroying our world – was inconceivable. I pitched with anxiety and tossed my bed sheets into a tangle at my feet. When I did finally manage to fall asleep, dreams pulled me beyond acceptable hallucinations and I would wake frightened and panting. In one dream, I was on a witness stand in a massive hollow of a courtroom. I was being accused of horrendous crimes against humanity. Every time I tried to defend myself the sounds of street clamour would emit from my mouth – car horns, air brakes. I tried desperately to be understood and pleaded for clemency but ended up fleeing the courtroom in terror as a supercharged steam-roller pursued me. I woke just as my body became pancake-thin.

After a long, drawn-out, night of tension, dawn broke but was barely discernible through the boiling clouds. I heard Rick somersaulting restlessly in his bed so I pushed my jumble of covers to the floor and tiptoed to his room. I poked my head in at the door.

"You awake?" I whispered.

"Yeah. Can't sleep."

"I don't suppose you somehow solved the riddle in the night?"

"No such luck."

"Are you still going to Hyde's Peak this afternoon?"

"Yeah. We have some guesses. We have to at least try."

I thought of asking Rick if we should tell Mom and Dad but left this proposal unspoken. I felt certain they had done the best anyone could have done. And besides, maybe it was better to not know.

XXXVIII

CASCADING RAIN FELL in drifting sheets as white talons of lightning lit up the sky. Rick left shortly after lunch. I wished him well but he didn't seem to hear me. I watched him from our front window as he disappeared down the street. My heart ached with each step he took in the driving torrent.

When thunder detonated like mortar fire, causing my home to shudder, my thoughts came back to Gwidon.

Maybe Rita was right. Maybe I was crazy. How could I possibly believe that someone who would not only imprison our dear friend but also threaten our very world might be anything other than pure evil? But yet...Gwidon's eyes. I swear I saw something else there. The others didn't see what I saw. I don't know. I guess it's all in how you look at things. It is all a matter of....Wait. Wait!

I ran up to my bedroom and began a frantic search for my copy of the riddle. But where was it? Oh no! Where was it? Pushing unwanted papers onto the floor, I rifled over what remained on my desk...desperate, frantic. When did I have it last? Yes! I knew where it was. I hadn't looked at it since Rita and I had had our fight. It was in my jacket pocket. I raced downstairs nearly colliding with Dad on the stairs.

"Alex? What's going on?"

I didn't answer but whipped the closet door open, recklessly flicking through our family's outerwear until I located my coat. Seizing it, I anxiously searched the right-hand pocket, then the left. There it was! I smoothed the paper out as well as I could and read it to myself, mouthing each word as I went. "That's it!"

XXXIX

"HOW ABOUT SPACE?"

"No, it doesn't go with 'I'm blind and yet have sight'."

"Time?"

"Not that either. The 'man and woman' stuff doesn't work with it."

"Maybe...matter?"

"I don't think so. Again, it doesn't work with 'I'm blind and yet have sight.'"

"What are we going to do?" Jerry cried out with worry. He, Rita and Rick were a wretched sight. Not only were they agonizing over solving the riddle and the unthinkable consequences of failure, they were tramping through a forested quagmire of mud in a thunderstorm, bodies bracing against the wind as crackling and flashes of light split the sky over their heads. They were greedy for anything that could remotely answer the riddle and stop this insanity. They slowed with each heartbreaking step closer to Lessie's tree.

"We've got to come up with something!" Rick shouted above the snarling wind.

Jerry yelled, "I think the closest we have to the answer is 'time'. It even goes with 'I'm blind and yet have sight' since with time, you gain knowledge – insight – you know, in-sight."

"Okay, Jerry. You win. It's the closest thing we have."

"All agreed then?" Jerry said turning to Rita.

"Yeah, I guess. It's just...I wish Alex..." Rita's voice trailed off. She hung her head even further against the storm.

Ultimately, the three of them did indeed make it to Lessie's arbutus tree, however haltingly. They arrived as winded and frightened as stampeded mustangs. They were still struggling for breath when Gwidon appeared through the bleak, dim light.

The air grew heavy with cannoning thunder as rolling clouds raced across the heavens. He was more stooped than before but he appeared eager to begin the proceedings. He glided with hurried intent to the stump of Lessie's tree, exactly opposite to Jerry who had moved protectively in front of Rita.

"Only three of you." It was an observation that for once sprang from his mouth and not from someplace distant. "No matter. The moment has come," he continued. "And now we will learn just how clever you really are. Will you provide me with the right answer to the final riddle and save your world or will you be wrong, signalling the end of everything you hold dear." He staggered slightly at that, but resettled himself quickly.

Rita, Jerry and Rick looked stricken.

He persisted, "After I recite the final riddle, I will allow you one minute to submit your answer." Without pausing for assent he began,

"I am both the sun and moon
When dark becomes the light.
All and none are part of me.
I'm blind and yet have sight.

Man and woman, young and old,
I'm here and also there.
I can't be found in every space
Yet I am everywhere.

I can die yet truly know
My immortality.
I am tied to future, past,
Where present longs to be.

Devil's pawn and angel's seed,
The yin and yang of me
Reminds me that I change with time
Yet your eyes won't see."

He concluded with, "What am I?" and looked grimly at the three kids.

"We won't need a minute." I said, stepping from behind the lone Douglas fir that thrived in the grove of arbutus.

"Alex!" the other kids shouted.

"Well," Gwidon looked at me coolly, "let's hear your answer and end this charade."

I took an audible breath, fortifying myself for the challenge, and began, "What is it that makes some see a moon while others see a sun? What is it that makes some see a man and some see a woman? What is it that makes some see a devil while others see an angel?" I glanced quickly at Rita before I concluded with, "Perspective."

The intensity of the storm diminished almost imperceptibly. Gwidon retreated slowly, never taking his eyes from mine, and then he stopped about 20 feet from where I stood. The suspense left us all open-mouthed, too stunned to move and unable to blink. Finally, he bowed his head, breaking the thread that entwined us. "So, you think you've solved the final riddle?" he said, without looking up.

I dug in my heels. "Yes. I'm sure of it."

He continued to look down – I couldn't see his face clearly – but his demeanour spoke to me. He seemed to be in despair, as if he were mourning something that he had deeply treasured – something that had become lost to him forever. He remained so for some time and I was beginning to believe that he had become trapped in his nightmare and had willed us away. But before I could consider what to do, his trance seemed to dissolve. He raised his eyes to meet mine and said, "You are correct."

I think we were all expecting the rain to finally stop, the menacing skies to instantly clear uncovering the sorely missed sun, and the winds to diminish into gentle ocean breezes but...we were very much mistaken. The rain continued to pour down – maybe not as hard as before but still torrential. The dark skies churned and the wind gusted with the same defeating force. I looked around in desperation, searching for any telltale sign of real improvement. Nothing. Then I lost it.

I spun around to face Gwidon and screamed, "Gwidon, stop it! Stop this blasted hurricane! This is heartless! I can't take this anymore! You promised Lessie that you would stop your manipulations once we solved the final riddle. We solved it. Live up to your side of the bargain! Stop this!"

Gwidon appeared unmoved. Staring coldly into my eyes, he finally spat, "I *have* relinquished my power over your weather. I did it as soon as you gave the correct answer."

"What? It's hardly changed. It's still horrific!"

"It is not my doing," said Gwidon weakly.

"Well, then whose doing is it?" I demanded.

Before Gwidon could answer, Rick moved forward and asked, "But, what about Lessie? You were supposed to free her from her tree."

Gwidon turned slowly and gazed at Rick pitilessly. "That was not part of the bargain." At that, he pitched forward but caught himself before he fell. He looked to be fading before our eyes.

"No! Alex solved the riddle. Lessie is supposed to be freed!" Rick yelled.

"Listen to me carefully," Gwidon said with pronounced effort, head down, steadying himself on a nearby branch. "I plucked a golden feather from that *Wila* swan and thereby gained her power. She will be imprisoned in her tree...forever. There is nothing you can do." He began to back away from us again – faltering but still lengthening the distance between us. He would have made it to his earthen lair had her voice not stopped his escape.

"Gwidon!" The sound of it seemed to scratch the very air.

We spun around as one. "Lessie!" I cried out. We all ran to her but I was in the lead – as is so often my way. My relief at seeing her welled up in my eyes. "Are you all right?"

Gwidon's quaking voice seemed to travel to my right shoulder as he demanded of Lessie, "How did you manage to escape?" Each syllable was clipped.

Her voice rang out clearly, "Gwidon, it was a charm. You see, a *Wila* elder, many years ago, told me a story about sister *Wila* swans who escaped permanent imprisonment when their golden wing feathers were plucked. By means of a combination of specially written spells, rare forest herbs and magic crystals, they were able to soften the curse, allowing them freedom but sadly in exchange, their special powers were extinguished. In effect, they became human. This charm bag," she said clutching the *ladanki* firmly, "also holds all those extraordinary elements. I was wearing it the day you attacked me."

We kids crowded around Lessie, laughing, crying, hugging, so relieved that at least we had Lessie back unscathed. Minutes passed and our joy remained undiminished until without warning, Lessie went ashen as she gazed past me where Gwidon had last been standing. Anguished, she broke from our sphere at speed.

When I turned, I saw Gwidon in a sickening heap on the saturated forest floor. Lessie was just reaching him when I heard her cry, "Gwidon! Gwidon, what is it?" I hastened to the scene.

"Les...I'm...sorry." I heard Gwidon utter weakly. He seemed to be searching Lessie's face for any sign of forgiveness. She cradled his head in her lap.

Lessie cried out, "I know, Gwidon. It's okay. I know you must have had a good reason. But Gwidon, please, how can I help you?"

"There's nothing you can do for me now. Lessie," he explored her face, "I...was so...desperate."

"Tell me Gwidon, tell me why you did this." She looked calm but dreadfully sad.

With what seemed like profound effort, Gwidon spoke what was to be his last riddle,

> "If the shroud of their misdeeds
> Remains as it is today,
> The sapphires on her emerald gown
> Will dim and fade away."

Lying back, yielding to his struggle, Gwidon died where he lay. Lessie, sobbing now, gently lowered him to the muddied ground where he appeared to gradually melt away, becoming one with the forest floor. Then, all trace of him vanished in an instant. Tears streamed down my face but I made no sound.

When Lessie stood up, we hugged, clinging to each other in our grief. I was aware that the others had gathered around us but they too remained silent. After a time, Lessie and I broke apart to face the others. Rita reached out to me and touched my arm tenderly. "I'm sorry," she said.

I grasped her hand firmly and said "Me too, Rita." Not another word was required to fully mend our friendship.

"Lessie, please help us to understand...all this," Jerry pleaded.

Lessie took a moment to compose herself and then said, "You humans don't realize it but there are forces at work that share your world with you – forces that are very powerful. As a

Wila, I occupied a place very close to your known world. You see, my kind serve you. My full name, Olesia even means 'defender of mankind'. Protecting you is our primary concern. Over time we have evolved, becoming more and more human with each passing generation and I think ultimately that is our destiny – to become human. That is why when I found out about the remarkable magic of the spells, herbs and crystals, I immediately set off on a quest for them, just in case I was ever attacked for my golden feathers."

She continued, "As I said, Gwidon was a *Vodianoi*. They too have incredible power. They are usually reclusive creatures that can live both in the ocean and on land but often reside in sunken ships or coral reefs, far from human eyes. But even with that said, the *Vodianoi* and humans often end up in close proximity to each other. Generally, when a human enters their area, the *Vodianoi* will move away undetected but I have to admit, over the last while this seems to be changing. Many have taken to defending their territory by sinking ships and frightening fishermen. Our roles as *Wilas* have become crucial. But Gwidon had never exhibited this kind of behaviour before. Don't get me wrong, he was always a pretty ill-tempered creature, but he was a loner and seemed to like it that way. To do what he did to me, he must have been very desperate."

Rick pitched in, "So Lessie, then why did he do it?"

"I don't know. I guess we need to solve his riddle to understand. Does anyone recall how the poem went?"

With his near photographic memory, Rick was a pro at this.

"If the shroud of their misdeeds
Remains as it is today,
The sapphires on her emerald gown
Will dim and fade away."

"So, what do you think? Any ideas? Why did Gwidon do this?" Lessie asked.

Then, out of the dark murkiness of the fading light came a familiar voice, "To stop global warming."

"Sasha!" I cried out. "What are you doing here?"

She walked slowly towards us, carefully threading her way through the muddy terrain. Raindrops fell from her mass of curly ginger hair.

"Your dad told me to look for you at The Peak," she replied.

"Sash, I..." I was befuddled. I didn't know what to say to her and then..."How long have you been here?" I was concerned about what all she had seen but, really, what did it matter now? It was over.

"I've been here for a while. Alex...I know everything. I need to explain..."

My mind was racing. Rick rallied while I stood back dazed. "What do you need to explain?"

"I know all about Gwidon...and Lessie. I've known for some time now."

"What! How?" I managed to croak.

"It all started with the earthquake. I sensed that it was not one of our everyday kinds of quakes. You see, I was once...Guys, this is really hard. I was once a...*Wila.*"

We let the word hang suspended for a few moments. Astonishment greeted me as I looked from face to face. Then Lessie, who had been reticent until now, unexpectedly stepped forward and said pensively, "Then that makes you...of course! I know all about you! You and your sister were the *Wila* sisters who gathered the charms and became human. You're responsible for my becoming human. Thank you." She smiled at Sasha and squeezed her hand warmly.

Rita said, "What? Wait, I don't understand. I thought...I guess I don't know what I thought."

"I'm sorry to have misled you," Sasha began. "It was tough. You were all so good to my family when we first arrived here. I really wanted you to like me, but I thought if you knew my past...well...you know..."

"Let me get this straight," said Jerry, shaking his head. "Sasha, you and Lex were once *Wilas*. You are now human because what just happened to Lessie, happened to you? Really?"

"Yes. My sister and I were captured by a *Vodianoi* who plucked a golden feather from each of us when we were in our swan state. He wanted to use our powers over storms in order to destroy the world. It happened just like with Lessie. But because we were wearing this," she pulled her leather *ladanki* from the inside of her shirt, "we survived and became humans. Sophia adopted us soon after." She clutched the charm bag tenderly in gratitude.

"So the earthquake, the riddles...all that happened to Lessie, happened to you and Lex?"

"Yes, Rita. Everything. It was a terrible experience, yes, though out of it all, my sister and I became human and we are happy about that. But, I guess the most important thing to come out of our ordeal is the awareness that we gained.

"The awareness?" I asked regaining some vestige of steadiness.

Sasha replied, "You know, Gwidon's final riddle. Why he did all this. Why the *Vodianoi* are so desperate. Global warming."

Lessie exhaled, "Of course. Global warming. Gwidon's very existence must have been in serious jeopardy."

"Yes," Sasha said. "I think you're right." She then explained to the rest of us, "Many *Vodianoi* live in coral reefs and unfortunately, their homes are deteriorating – largely due to a warming and increasingly acidic ocean caused by rising levels of carbon dioxide. This, coupled with the fact that storms are becoming more severe due to the rising temperatures, is making life in our oceans perilous. Plus, there are the complications of overfishing, coastal development, and pollution. I suspect Gwidon had been made sick by industrial run-off. And he also observed that he wasn't the only one suffering. He must have hated what he saw happening to himself and his fellow ocean dwellers and I guess he just...couldn't take it any longer." At this she paused, tears welling up, and bent her head solemnly.

At her mention of Gwidon, I gazed at his final resting place, a spot void of any trace of him, save in my heart. A desolation settled over me as the steady rain battered the land. It was then that I resolved that his death would not be in vain. I would do my part to help save the oceans.

Sasha resumed. "Since becoming human, Lex and I have upheld our pledge of being... well...defenders of mankind – just in a different way. You see, the health of our oceans is vital to the planet. They supply us with so many vital systems that our very world remains habitable because of them. And combating global warming is a huge part of our mission to protect humans."

"Wait. Defenders of mankind? Funny. Lessie told us that is exactly what Olesia means," I said.

"Well...what do you think Sasha and Lex mean?"

"You're kidding! Defenders of mankind?"

"And Alex. I have news for you. Guess what your name means!"

"Are you serious?"

"Yep. But obviously, all names don't mean the same thing nor do all names necessarily even have a meaning."

"Well," I said, "What about Gwidon. Did his name have a meaning?"

And now Lessie stepped forward and spoke. "Yes it did. Life."

XL

"BILLY! BILLY! WILL you stop?" I was shouting in vain. That dog! He raced along the ocean's edge, blissfully ignoring me.

"Oh, just let him run, Alex. He was so cooped up this winter."

My mom and I walked leisurely, drinking in the sun's warmth and the seaside air and stopping now and then to examine the occasional bits of shell and rock washed up on the extended shoreline. It was a glorious west coast day at the beach – sparkling bright and resplendent. We had left Rick in the shade on our backyard deck reading *The Medusa and the Snail*. Dad was also in the backyard but he was taking a nap on a hammock tied between two Garry Oaks.

But, sadly even the rapture we felt in that sunbeam loveliness could not hide the shattered remnants of last winter. Telltale signs – eroded shore banks, tracks of downed trees, and flood-devastated lowlands – all foretold of a landscape that would be forever altered.

Three weeks after Lessie moved in with Sasha and her family, we experienced the most rainfall in a single day in recorded history. That had been in December. Another windstorm rocked the west coast soon afterward, knocking out power all through the area, downing countless trees and causing massive property damage.

I guess the only positive note to come out of all this misfortune is that global warming has become a universal concern. People have become better informed about the consequences of their actions and they are changing accordingly. Recycling, buying local, joining environmental groups, buying energy-efficient appliances, undergoing energy audits – the list goes on – all have become pretty commonplace.

Governments are finally taking the issue more seriously as well. More aggressive greenhouse gas emissions targets, wide-sweeping climate change research studies, and international agreements to establish a low-carbon economy have all been pledged – to name a few of the recent initiatives.

And on a personal level, me and a bunch of other kids in the area (ex-*Wila* and otherwise) have started our own club to spread awareness – not only of the global warming issue but also of the plight of our oceans. Our club is called The Defenders. Pretty cool, huh?

"Oh look, Alex!" Mom was pointing to something swimming just off shore. "I think it's a seal."

I followed the direction of her gaze. Yes, it looked like a seal but...I don't know. It could easily have been something else. Something, perhaps...mythical?

Because, really, well...anything's possible.

APPENDIX A: OUR OCEANS ARE IN CRISIS

WHAT FOLLOWS IS a bit of information The Defenders Club uncovered about our oceans.

The health of our oceans is deteriorating and human activity is fundamentally to blame. Six billion people populate our planet and some experts forecast that by 2050 this figure could climb to as many as nine billion. With such high population levels, our consumption of the world's resources greatly surpasses that of any other species on Earth. This, in combination with our highly developed technologies, makes the alteration and exploitation of our natural world almost effortless. Unfortunately, too often, this is to the detriment of existing ecologies.

Widespread development of coastal cities around the world is methodically devastating the natural environment of complex systems of flora and fauna, rendering recovery virtually impossible. Estuaries and wetlands which serve as nurseries to numerous land and marine life forms disappear every year as casualties of urban encroachment. Toxic pollutants, grease and oil from various human activities run off our streets, flowing ultimately into our oceans, killing marine life. The natural habitats of countless species are being transformed and generally obliterated by the dredging and deepening of harbours, as well as by off-shore drilling, aquaculture and the construction of dams and dykes.

Sea life that once thrived in our oceans is also in grave peril due to overfishing. In recent years, fishery technological advancements have developed with escalating efficiency and industrialized fishing fleets have grown in numbers exponentially. Consequently, fish of virtually all species are being caught in numbers that cannot possibly be sustained by our oceans. Ninety per cent of big fish (sharks, tuna, snapper, marlin, etc.) for example, have been extracted from our oceans in the last 50 years. To exacerbate this crisis, many tons of smaller fish are being captured and supplied to fish farms every year, leaving the numbers of smaller fish greatly depleted.

Furthermore, some modern fishing techniques not only enable the fishing industry to catch more fish but also expose other marine life forms to added jeopardy. By-catch operations capture many superfluous creatures alongside desired species. Many of those unwanted species often die before they are thrown back into the ocean. Tens of thousands of birds and turtles, more than 300,000 whales, dolphins and porpoises and more than 20 million tons of fish are killed needlessly as by-catch in industrial fishing operations each year.

Dead zones (areas of our oceans that are devoid of life) are becoming more prevalent. As they try to meet the escalating demands of a growing population, agricultural operations produce more and more nitrates and phosphates. Regrettably, these course downward, seeping into rivers and eventually come to rest in our oceans. When this occurs, oxygen is effectively removed from the water. Sea life in these waters cannot survive without oxygen and must either swim away or die. This is one way in which dead zones are created. The number of dead zones in our oceans has increased from 50 a decade ago to more than 150 today.

But perhaps the most worrisome development facing our oceans is the fact that they are becoming warmer. Our once healthy atmosphere is thickening due chiefly to human generated carbon dioxide. Infrared radiation that would once escape our atmosphere is becoming trapped by our thickened atmosphere thereby increasing the Earth and her oceans' temperature. This is the phenomenon called global warming. Even modest increases in ocean temperature can have crushing results.

Ocean warming is responsible for coral bleaching and the subsequent death of coral reefs found around the world. Zooxanthellae are organisms that have a symbiotic relationship with coral and provide their host coral with food and oxygen. When ocean temperatures rise even as little as one to two degrees, this relationship breaks down and the zooxanthellae are often expelled, resulting in coral bleaching and in many cases the death of the coral. During the hottest year recorded (2005) there was a mass coral mortality event. Today, 20 per cent of our world's coral reefs have been devastated and a further 24 per cent are in danger of imminent collapse. Since coral reefs act as our oceans' rainforests, a multitude of other ecosystems depend on them and may consequently be brought to extinction if these warming trends continue unchecked.

In addition to warming, our oceans are also becoming more acidic. Almost half of all carbon dioxide produced by human beings since the dawn of the Industrial Revolution has been absorbed by our oceans. As a result, they are becoming more acidic. This acidity further damages weakened coral reefs, contributes to the number and size of our oceans' dead zones, decimates populations of species at the bottom of our food chain and damages the shells of mussels, oysters and clams.

With warmer oceans, storms are being generated more frequently and with mounting ferocity causing major flooding, damage to property, habitat destruction and loss of life in areas all over the world. In addition to this, the polar ice caps are melting causing sea levels to rise thereby worsening this already destructive and dangerous phenomenon. If the polar ice were to completely melt, millions of people worldwide would be forced from their homes as we would experience sea levels up to 20 feet above current levels.

If the polar ice caps continue to melt unabated, the gradual slowing and potential stoppage of the movement of our vital ocean currents could transpire. Water that remains after evaporation in the North Atlantic for example, is saltier and therefore heavier than other water. As it sinks, it powers the thermohaline circulation that causes cold water currents to flow southward toward the Eastern seaboard of North America and warm water currents to flow northward toward Western Europe. If the ice on Greenland were to melt, local waters could become so diluted that the movement of saltwater to the ocean floor could slow or conceivably stop. If this were to happen, the north and south flowing ocean currents would cease their progress and incredibly, an ice age could develop.

Our oceans are home to 80 per cent of all life found on our planet. They provide the Earth with oxygen, energy, proteins, nutrients and minerals and are responsible for driving our weather systems. In effect, it is our oceans that keep our world habitable. As overwhelming as the threats to our oceans and our planet may be, we must work toward reversing the damage we have wrought before it is too late. By educating ourselves to the consequences of our actions and subsequently initiating tenable changes to our practices as human beings, we will have a much greater likelihood of extending the gifts our world provides for generations to come.

What You and Your Parents Can Do To Help

Initiate Change with a Wallet

- **Buy a more fuel-efficient vehicle** to reduce your carbon dioxide emissions.

- **Buy environmentally friendly merchandise.**

- **Buy fresh food instead of frozen** since frozen food requires much more energy to produce.

- **Buy less heavily packaged products** to reduce your household waste.

- **Buy locally grown foods** to save fuel in transport.

- **Buy only sustainable seafood.**

- **Buy organic foods and products.**

- **Buy rechargeable batteries.**

- **Buy recycled paper products** since it requires much less energy to produce them. This would also prevent the loss of many trees.

- **Choose energy-efficient appliances.**

  o **Ceiling Fans**. Air conditioners require considerably more energy to operate than ceiling fans.

  o **Clothes Washer**. Energy-efficient washers use much less water than conventional models. High speed motors reduce the length of the spin cycle and remove more water from your clothes thereby reducing drying time and energy consumption. The use of the cold water cycle saves energy as well.

  o **Dishwasher**. Energy-efficient dishwashers require less heated water to operate therefore less energy is consumed. And when you allow your dishes to air dry and only operate your dishwasher when it is full, you reduce your household energy consumption further.

  o **Furnace**. Installing an energy-efficient furnace can significantly reduce your home energy consumption. Ensuring your furnace is maintained and its filters are cleaned or changed regularly also helps considerably.

  o **Home office equipment**. An energy-efficient computer in sleep mode uses much less energy than a conventional model. Energy-efficient laptops use even less energy due to their size.

  o **Refrigerators**. Energy-efficient refrigerators limit heat loss, are more temperature precise and are better insulated than standard models.

  o **Windows and doors**. All energy-efficient windows and doors eliminate drafts and condensation. Storm windows and doors offer considerable benefits as well.

- **Consider the effect your investments have on the environment.**

- **Cut down or eliminate meat from your diet.** Cattle produce large quantities of the greenhouse gas methane.

- **Don't buy products made from endangered or threatened species.**

- **Use paper instead of plastic products whenever possible.**

Initiate Change with Actions

- **Adopt a beach, stream, road, etc.**

- **Carpool whenever possible.**

- **Clean up your local beaches and your neighbourhood regularly.**

- **Conserve water.** Take shorter showers and turn off the tap when you brush your teeth.

- **Consider car sharing.** Car sharing organizations provide members with access to a community car.

- **Convert to renewable energy** such as wind or solar.

- **Dispose of chemicals responsibly.**

- **Dive responsibly.** Never remove shells or coral from their environment.

- **Don't fly as often.**

- **Don't waste food.** Save leftovers.

- **Drive with fuel economy in mind**. To save weight and fuel, remove all unnecessary items from your vehicle.

- **Fix broken items instead of throwing them away.**

- **Sign up to have your home undergo an energy audit.** This will help you identify energy inefficiency within your home.

- **If you have an extra refrigerator or freezer, ensure that it is not overloaded, that its door seals securely and that its coils are kept clean.**

- **If you water your lawn or garden, ensure it is done either in the evening or early in the morning** to minimize evaporation.

- **If you will be away from your home for more than three days, remember to turn your thermostat to its lowest setting**. Or, in the case of an air-conditioning unit, set it at a temperature higher than you'd normally tolerate.

- **Install a programmable thermostat.** This will automatically lower the heat at night and raise it for you in the morning.

- **Install dual flush toilets and other water saving methods** to conserve water.

- **Install wall plate insulators and safety caps.**

- **Keep your vehicle's tires properly inflated.**

- **Make a compost heap from garden and household scraps** to fertilize your garden.

- **Only take pictures when exploring nature.** Tread lightly and leave nothing behind.

- **Plant a garden.**

- **Plant a tree.** The shade it provides could also help keep your home cooler in the summer.

- **Practise safe and responsible boating.**

- **Protect your environment from invasive species.**

- **Reduce your emissions by taking public transit, walking or biking.**

- **Regularly maintain your vehicle** to improve fuel economy while reducing your emissions.

- **Remember the 3 R's of helping the environment: Reduce, Reuse, and Recycle.**

- **Replace incandescent light bulbs with compact fluorescent light bulbs.**

- **Return empty bottles and cans for a refund.**

- **Simplify.** Reduce your consumerism and pass on the household items that you are not using to others.

- **Telecommute from home if possible.**

- **Turn off the lights, TV, radio, etc.** when you leave a room.

- Unplug electronic devices, appliances, etc. when not in use.

- Use a clothesline to air dry clothing whenever possible.

- Use only safe pesticides and herbicides on your lawn and garden.

- Use re-usable dishes and cups instead of disposables.

- Use re-usable shopping and gift bags.

- When possible, cover cooking pots so that food cooks faster. Use stainless steel cookware.

- Winterize your home by insulating your attic, basement and crawl space to R50 and applying caulking and weather-stripping around windows and doors.

- Wrap your water heater in an insulating blanket.

Initiate Change with Your Voice

- Encourage everyone to think globally and act locally.

- Encourage your friends, family, co-workers, etc. to reduce emissions.

- Encourage your government to fight for the environment by writing to your local, provincial and federal representatives.

- **Join and support environmental groups.**

- **Organize events** to spread awareness of environmental issues and raise funds for causes.

- **Read more about environmental issues to educate yourself and others.**

Sources and Recommended Reading

Clover, Charles. *The End of the Line: How Overfishing Is Changing the World and What We Eat.* New York, NY: New Press, 2006

Earle, Sylvia A. *The World Is Blue: How Our Fate and the Ocean's Are One.* Washington, DC: National Geographic Society, 2009

Ellis, Richard. *On Thin Ice: The Changing World of the Polar Bear.* New York, NY: Alfred A. Knopf, 2009

Ellis, Richard. *The Empty Ocean.* Washington, DC: Island Press, 2003

Fujita, Rod. *Heal the Ocean: Solutions for Saving Our Seas.* Gabriola Island, BC: New Society Publishers, 2003

Gore, Al. *An Inconvenient Truth: The Planetary Emergency of Global Warming and What We Can Do About It.* New York, NY: Rodale Books, 2006

Hansen, James. *Storms of My Grandchildren: The Truth about the Coming Climate Catastrophe and Our Last Chance to Save Humanity.* New York, NY: Bloomsbury, USA, 2009

Helvarg, David. *50 Ways to Save the Ocean*. Makawao, Maui, HI: Inner Ocean Publishing, Inc., 2006

Mazur, Laurie Ann. *Beyond the Numbers: A Reader on Population, Consumption and the Environment*. Washington, DC: Island Press, 1994

Mitchell, Alanna. *Seasick: Ocean Change and the Extinction of Life on Earth*. Chicago, IL: University Of Chicago Press, 2009

Norse, Elliott. Marine *Conservation Biology: The Science of Maintaining the Sea's Biodiversity*. Washington, DC: Island Press, 2005

Pollack, Henry. *A World Without Ice*. New York, NY: Penguin Group, 2009

Roberts, Callum. *The Unnatural History of the Sea*. Washington, DC: Island Press, 2007

Safina, Carl. *Song for the Blue Ocean: Encounters Along the World's Coasts and Beneath the Seas*. New York, NY: Henry Holt and Company, Inc., 1997

Sapp, Jan. *What is Natural: Coral Reef Crisis*. New York, NY: Oxford University Press, 1999

Schmidt, Gavin and Joshua Wolfe. *Climate Change: Picturing the Science*. New York, NY: W. W. Norton & Company, Inc., 2009

Ward, Peter D. *Under a Green Sky: Global Warming, the Mass Extinctions of the Past, and What They Can Tell Us About Our Future*. New York, NY: HarperCollins Publishers, 2007

Wilson, Edward O. *The Future of Life*. New York, NY: Alfred A Knopf, 2002

Websites

David Suzuki Foundation. http:www.davidsuzuki.org

Global Issues. http:www.globalissues.org

Greenpeace International. http:www.greenpeace.org

International Union for Conservation of Nature. http:www. iucn.org

Mother Jones. http:www.motherjones.com

Natural Resources Canada - Energy Star in Canada.
http:www.energystar.gc.ca

Natural Resources Canada - Office of Energy Efficiency.
http:www.oee.nrcan.gc.ca

Ocean Conservancy. http:www.oceanconservancy.org

Science Progress. http:www.scienceprogress.org

Sierra Club. http:www.sierraclub.org

World Wildlife Fund. http:www.worldwildlifefund.org

ABOUT THE AUTHOR

Chris Manning's first book, George and Condi: The Last Decayed is a politically charged collection of poems inspired by events which transpired over the first ten years of this century. Her second book, Beaver Tales and a Canada Goosing, is a candid series of poems representing a distinctively Canadian perspective on world events, the current state of western society and on Canada itself with parody thrown in for good measure. In her three-part series, *To the Shore of a Child's Ocean*, she portrays one Canadian family's journey through the dynamic educational culture that is homeschooling. *Vodianoi* is the companion novel to the second installment of this series but is intended for all fantasy loving youth. Chris Manning and her family have made Vancouver Island their home since 1996.

ArtisanPacificPublishing@gmail.com

Made in the USA
Charleston, SC
20 August 2011